One Warm, Wet Kiss.

Make that one helluva kiss, Anthony silently amended as he stared at Zoe, who was flushed and naked and alluring and begging him to get naked, too. As her big brown eyes flicked over him in awe, he felt something hot and dangerous luring him on.

He gasped. "This is crazy."

She moved against him. "I don't know what I want," Zoe said, her voice lower, sexier.

"Well, maybe I do." His finger traced along her soft cheek, down her throat, down, down, circling over each nipple until they peaked into pert little beads of desire.

She shuddered. "You think so, huh? Let's see if you're still as hunky out of those clothes as you are in them."

Then she was peeling him out of his shirt, leaning into him, her slim fingers flying over those shirt buttons. She yanked his shirt off his shoulders, then caressed sculpted muscle.

Giggling, Zoe ran her hands down his naked spine. "I want to hate you. Did you know that's been my ambition for nine years?"

"Mine, too." Anthony pulled her closer. "We're not doing too good."

Dear Reader,

’Tis the season to read six passionate, powerful and provocative love stories from Silhouette Desire!

Savor *A Cowboy & a Gentleman* (#1477), December’s MAN OF THE MONTH, by beloved author Ann Major. A lonesome cowboy rekindles an old flame in this final title of our MAN OF THE MONTH promotion. MAN OF THE MONTH has had a memorable fourteen-year run and now it’s time to make room for other exciting innovations, such as DYNASTIES: THE BARONES, a Boston-based Romeo-and-Juliet continuity with a happy ending, which launches next month, and—starting in June 2003—Desire’s three-book sequel to Silhouette’s out-of-series continuity THE LONE STAR COUNTRY CLUB. Desire’s popular TEXAS CATTLEMAN’S CLUB continuity also returns in 2003, beginning in November.

This month DYNASTIES: THE CONNELLYS concludes with *Cherokee Marriage Dare* (#1478) by Sheri WhiteFeather, a riveting tale featuring a former Green Beret who rescues the youngest Connelly daughter from kidnappers. Award-winning, bestselling romance novelist Rochelle Alers debuts in Desire with *A Younger Man* (#1479), the compelling story of a widow’s sensual renaissance. Barbara McCauley’s *Royally Pregnant* (#1480) offers a fabulous finale to Silhouette’s cross-line CROWN AND GLORY series, while a feisty rancher corrals the sexy cowboy-next-door in *Her Texas Temptation* (#1481) by Shirley Rogers. And a blizzard forces a lone wolf to deliver his hometown sweetheart’s infant in *Baby & the Beast* (#1482) by Laura Wright.

Here’s hoping you find all six of these supersensual Silhouette Desire titles in your Christmas stocking.

Enjoy!

Joan Marlow Golan

Joan Marlow Golan
Senior Editor, Silhouette Desire

Ann Major

A COWBOY & A GENTLEMAN

Published by Silhouette Books
America's Publisher of Contemporary Romance

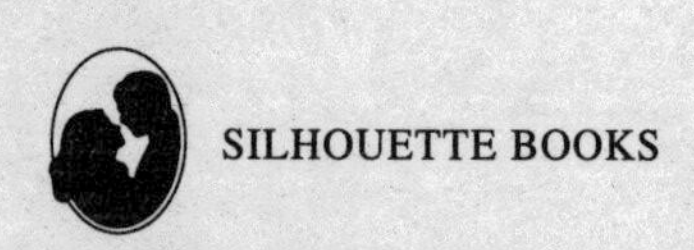

ISBN 0-373-76477-4

A COWBOY & A GENTLEMAN

This edition published by arrangement with Harlequin Books S.A.

Visit Silhouette at www.eHarlequin.com

Printed in U.S.A.

Books by Ann Major

Silhouette Desire

Dream Come True #16
Meant To Be #35
Love Me Again #99
The Wrong Man #151
Golden Man #198
Beyond Love #229
In Every Stranger's Face #301
What This Passion Means #331
**Passion's Child* #445
**Destiny's Child* #451
**Night Child* #457
**Wilderness Child* #535
**Scandal's Child* #564
**The Goodbye Child* #648
A Knight in Tarnished Armor #690
Married to the Enemy #716
†*Wild Honey* #805
†*Wild Midnight* #819
†*Wild Innocence* #835
The Accidental Bride #889
A Cowboy Christmas #967
The Accidental Bodyguard #1003
**Nobody's Child* #1105
Love Me True #1213
Midnight Fantasy #1304
Cowboy Fantasy #1375
A *Cowboy & a Gentleman* #1477

*Children of Destiny
†Something Wild

Silhouette Intimate Moments

Seize the Moment #54

Silhouette Romance

Wild Lady #90
A Touch of Fire #150

Silhouette Special Edition

Brand of Diamonds #83
Dazzle #229
The Fairy Tale Girl #390

Silhouette Books

Silhouette Christmas Stories 1990
"Santa's Special Miracle"

Silhouette Summer Sizzlers 1992
"The Barefoot Enchantress"

Birds, Bees and Babies 1994
"The Baby Machine"

Silhouette Summer Sizzlers 1995
"Fancy's Man"

Montana Mavericks Weddings 1998
"A Bride, Baby and All"

Matters of the Heart 2001
"You're My Baby"

ANN MAJOR

lives in Texas with her husband of many years and is the mother of three grown children. She has a master's degree from Texas A&M at Kingsville, Texas, and is a former English teacher. She is a founding board member of the RWA and a frequent speaker at writers' groups.

Ann loves to write; she considers her ability to do so a gift. Her hobbies include hiking in the mountains, sailing, ocean kayaking, traveling and playing the piano. But most of all she enjoys her family.

To Karen Solem, a truly great agent,
who was there for me long before she was my agent.

And to Tara Gavin, my wonderful editor,
who has faith in me even when I don't,
and who has infinite patience and wisdom, too.

And to Ted, for loving me and giving me the most
wonderful three weeks of my life in Greece.

And to Greece...

ACKNOWLEDGMENT

I need to thank Patience Smith
for telling me about her job as an editor
and Caleb Huett for telling me what it's like
to be eight years old.

Prologue

What's a girl to do when she wakes up in bed married to the wrong man?

"I can't face Tony! I just can't!"

Zoe Creighton dashed up the ladder and flung herself onto a heap of hay in the loft. Her heart pounding, she moved into a crouch and peered through a crack in the barn's siding. She saw the snug, low roofs of Aunt Patty's ranch house and the windmill glinting in the late-afternoon sun below.

Anthony's truck was parked out front. The white cloud of dust that had plumed behind him when he'd driven up the caliche road so fast—and sent her flying out the back screen door in terror—hadn't quite settled over the thorny South Texas brush country.

The air was sweet with the familiar perfume of the barn—horses, oats, hay, leather and dung. She could almost smell the bluebonnets that had turned the mesquite-studded pasture closest to the house into a sea of undulating blue blossoms.

"Oh, if only…if only I could turn back time, just twenty-four hours…. I'd do it all so differently."

Zoe squeezed her eyes shut and tried to make herself believe that everything was the same. Only nothing was. Nothing would ever be the same again.

"Good Lord! What have you gone and done to yourself, Zoe Creighton?" she said aloud. "And Creighton's not even your last name anymore."

Brushing at her lashes, Zoe stared at the huge diamond on her left hand. Then, as if she still couldn't believe it was there, she held it up to that crack in the barn siding, so that the gaudy jewel shot white bits of glitter onto the wooden walls.

The ring was real all right. Only it was the wrong man's ring.

Quickly she fisted the hand and hid it behind her back.

Aunt Patty was always saying she was flighty and impulsive as a chicken. Zoe was only twenty, only a mere junior at the nearby branch of Texas A & M University, but she felt as if her life was already over.

"Stupid. That's what I am."

The barn door rolled, and just as she'd feared he might, Tony Duke stomped inside on a burst of blinding light, shouting her name so loudly the horses below snickered restlessly, their hooves clanging against the stall floors.

She stiffened. "Oh, why can't you just go on home and leave well enough alone?" she whispered to herself. "I came here to hide from you, you big, handsome idiot."

Used to be, when she'd see his truck roaring up to her gate, she'd rushed out to meet him.

"I can't face you. I can't tell you. Not after what we did here in this loft together yesterday," she added. The mere thought of her naked, virginal body under his warmed her like a fever.

"You have to tell him."

How had Tony known the exact moment Duncan had brought her back from Vegas?

Maybe if Tony couldn't find her, he'd give up and leave. Fearfully she peeped over the edge of the loft and stared down at his shiny, black head.

No doubt, because of the rodeo, he wore a red cowboy shirt and jeans. His wide shoulders made him look tough. The way he cocked his head back, so that his chin jutted out, made him look arrogant. He was so handsome every girl in the surrounding counties was in love with him. Why had he chosen her? Zoe had such a poor opinion of herself she'd never quite believed he loved her.

He strode about, throwing open the stall doors, calling the horses by their individual names as he searched for her.

"Give up, baby. Please…just go," Zoe whispered.

He slammed a stall door so hard she gasped. She must've jumped, too, because bits of hay sifted down and landed on his thick shoulders and black head.

"Oh, dear."

He peeled one out of his hair and another off his red shoulder. "So, you're up in the loft, are you?" He sounded angry but flirty, too.

"Don't you dare come up here! I don't want to talk to you ever again," she cried.

"You're wrong about that, baby," he rasped, striding toward the ladder. "Now, don't be shy."

Her heart pounded every time his boots struck a wooden rung. At the thought of facing him, she felt tears burning behind her eyelids. She was so scared, she began to shake.

First his big, tanned hands came into view, then the rest of him. For a long moment he simply stared at her. As always his carved face was dark and gorgeous, his sweet smile bold and white.

"I love that dress."

Her blue gingham.

"You're still wearing it," he said gently.

She remembered what he'd said yesterday when he'd first seen her in it, before he'd touched her, and her stomach did a crazy somersault.

She blushed. Everything was different now.

"Just go," she whispered, frantic now, as she backed toward the wall.

"Your aunt said you were in here. She seemed in some sort of snit."

No way could Zoe answer that.

"I missed you last night, baby. Looked everywhere for you at the rodeo. I'm sorry. It's not like you think." His voice was as soft as velvet, and because of what she'd done, it wrenched every part of her.

Could he be telling the truth? No!

"Too late to be sorry," she muttered, remembering what she'd done. "I'm sorry, too, and I have as much to be sorry about as you do."

"Rene means nothing to me," he whispered, slinging a denim-clad leg onto the rough flooring of the loft.

"That's not what she said."

He laughed. "She thinks she's hot. She's inclined to stretch the truth."

Her best friend, Rene, had been after him for years.

When he stood up, he loomed over Zoe in the tiny loft. Her fear made him look even taller and more dangerously formidable than yesterday when his nearness and gentleness had made her melt.

"I don't care what she said, and neither will you when I'm done kissing you," he whispered.

"There won't be any more kissing. Not here. We already got ourselves into way too much trouble."

"How come you ran away after we made love?" he whispered.

"I was scared. I couldn't believe we did it."

"Then you got up your courage and came back and found me with Rene."

"How could you go from me to her?"

"I couldn't. I didn't. I love you."

"That's just a word. I saw what I saw. She was all over you."

"Baby, I won't say Rene didn't give it her best shot."

"Are you saying that you didn't—"

One side of his mouth curved downward, and he gave her that lopsided smile she'd loved to think belonged to her alone. He was so tall and dark, so undeniably handsome. Just looking at him made her remember the thrill of his muscular body on top of hers. *Oh, dear.*

"I'm saying that I didn't," he replied.

She almost believed him. Her doubts shredded her heart.

In spite of everything, she still loved him.

"Last night I was a virgin."

"And that means everything to me."

Nervousness tightened her throat. Last night seemed so long ago. She couldn't tell him what she'd done. She couldn't.

"Go. Just go," she whispered.

"Darlin'," he murmured in that voice she'd thought belonged to her alone, too.

When he edged closer, she went still. When less than an inch separated his mouth from hers, he bent his head to hers and kissed her softly.

Before she could think, her mouth opened. His hands slid into her hair, down her neck, and then all over her just like they had twenty-four short hours ago. A lifetime ago.

"This time I'll go slower," he whispered, his breathing sounding rougher after just that one kiss.

For a second the tenderness and passion in his lips and hands made her forget everything that had gone so terribly wrong. It was as if it were all a bad dream. Now she was wide awake and Tony was here, and everything was all right again.

She wasn't the shy, plain girl, who read all the time. She wasn't in over her head, dating the most popular and the most handsome guy anywhere around Shady Lomas. Rene hadn't stolen him right after they'd made love for the first time. Zoe hadn't gone to the pig races and bumped into the town's most scandalous citizen, Tony's uncle Duncan Duke.

Uncle Duncan. If only he hadn't been so understanding.

Anthony's hands were sliding around her shoulders, down her spine to press her closer and kiss her again. The images of Duncan driving her around on those back-country roads in his red Cadillac blurred.

Was it only this morning that she'd awakened so woozily in Vegas next to the man? Reaching for him, she'd whispered Anthony's name only to scream when Duncan Duke had slung back the sheets and laughed at her.

"Mrs. Duke, when you wake up next to your bridegroom, and you don't know his name, it was a damn good wedding night."

She'd blinked at the old reprobate in horror. Good wedding night? How could he say such a thing? What was he talking about? His gray goatee had blurred. "We're not married! You're old enough to be my father."

He'd lifted her left hand. "That didn't bother you last night. Remember? Broken heart? Rene? My, but you were hell-bent on revenge."

He'd laughed again.

Revenge? No! She hadn't remembered the wedding or the wedding night at all. Indeed, she hadn't remembered anything much but those little pigs racing their hearts out for chocolate cookies stuffed with vanilla cream. She'd drunk a few beers while Duncan had listened to her talk about his nephew, Tony, in between races. Then when the races were over, Duncan had driven her around in his Cadillac and had taken her up in his plane. After that, the rest of the night was a total blur.

"We flew all the way to Vegas?"

"That and more." Duncan had kissed her left hand and made his obscene ring sparkle. "You proposed to me, said it would put the town in an uproar and take my arrogant nephew down a peg or two."

"I thought you loved Aunt Patty."

"Nothing like a surprise or two!"

"Take me home! This didn't happen! You aren't my husband!"

He'd climbed out of bed stark naked and produced the appropriate documents; photographs of the ceremony, too.

She'd stared at the photograph of herself wrapped in Duncan's arms and felt sick. "I kissed you? What else—"

The leer he'd given her had scared her. "No," she'd whispered. "Please, don't tell me!"

"I can fill you in on the details any time."

Well, maybe she was home again. But nothing could change the facts. She was married to Duncan Duke.

Worse! Here she was in her aunt's barn kissing her husband's nephew, Anthony, and moaning with pleasure, too. This was a nightmare! Only she wasn't going to wake up! This was a real life nightmare.

Placing her hands against Anthony's wide chest, she shoved. When he finally let her go, she fell backward a little.

Slowly she lifted Duncan Duke's big ring into a stream of light that sifted through a crack in the wooden siding. Turning her hand, she made sparks of light hit Tony's carved face.

Anthony squinted, but his dark eyes were on her wet, bruised lips and not on his uncle's ring.

"I've done something that can't be undone," she whispered brokenly. "It's like a nightmare. Only it's worse. 'Cause it's real. I can't believe I did it. But I was so hurt. I guess I wanted to get back at you."

"Baby, I love you so much there's nothing in the

whole world I couldn't forgive you. I've always loved you. Since you were a little girl in the sixth grade with those long, beautiful red braids. Why can't you ever just believe me?"

"'Cause I'm me and you're you. 'Cause I'm not popular or pretty."

"I've told you and told you that's all in your mind. You can be anything you want to be and have anybody you want."

Almost absently she moved her hand so that the diamond flashed fire across the coarse boards of the wall. "I was so mad at you about Rene that I ran off...and...and...well, I guess I got married. Truth to tell...I don't really remember."

"Married?" He grabbed her hand hard and stared at the ring on her finger. His mouth worked, but he couldn't speak. His eyes went cold as he studied her white face.

"I married your uncle Duncan," she murmured, staring down at his black boots.

"You what?" He cupped her chin and lifted it, so that he could look her square in the eye.

"I—"

"That old bastard's older than your daddy would be if he was alive! He's a scoundrel."

"I know that!"

"He was supposed to be courtin' your aunt Patty. The whole town watched him drive out here in that damned red Cadillac he wouldn't be able to afford if he hadn't stolen our land."

"Well, he married me. I don't know why he did it, but he did it."

"Because he's a bastard."

Usually the term bastard was an insult, but in this

case it was also a pertinent fact. Duncan Duke, who had long thrived on being Shady Lomas's number-one bad egg, had been born a bastard and pretended he was proud as hell about it.

Tony's grandfather, Harry Duke, had had two families, one on the wrong side of the sheets and one on the right side. He'd loved them both with a powerful passion.

Henrietta Duke, Harry's *legitimate* daughter, was Tony's strong-willed, straitlaced mother. Harry hadn't married wild, pretty Eva, Duncan's mother, but when Old Harry had finally died, he'd left the best part of the family ranch to his legitimate daughter, the stern Henrietta, his rightful heir.

Only, fate had played a wild card. Oil and gas had been discovered on the worthless marshland that fun-loving Duncan had inherited. Soon Duncan had become the richest man in three counties—three very huge Texas counties. He'd been buying land ever since his first gas wells had come in, and flaunting his wealth whenever possible. He'd had several wives, each one younger and prettier than the last. This was very upsetting to the town folk and especially to his two daughters.

Henrietta, who'd been hard-pressed to make it in the cattle business during the last drought, had been forced to sell Duncan the family's historical, red-roofed ranch house. She'd also sold him most of her prime ranch land, land that she leased back from him so she and Tony could run their herd on it.

"Every acre your husband owns should be mine—especially the house!"

"Is that all you care about—the house and land? The ranch?"

"What did you care about when you married my uncle Duncan?" Anthony's hair was blue-black; his face a livid, scary white.

"You slept with Rene, so it's your fault I went crazy and woke up married. I...I really don't remember it all exactly."

"You don't remember? Like hell! Let's get one thing straight! I did not sleep with Rene! But I will now! You were right! You've done something I'll never forgive! Neither will the town or the county! Neither will Uncle Duncan's daughters, my precious half cousins, Lana and Sue Ellen. They'll tear you to pieces. Why do you think he married you—to get back at all of us, that's why!"

Suddenly Anthony grabbed her by the shoulders.

"What are you doing?"

To her surprise, he circled her with his arms. "Don't I get to kiss the bride?"

She twisted and uttered an infuriated cry. "Not if you hate me so much!"

"There's no *if* about it, darlin'." He caught both her hands and held on tight, forcing her back against the wall. He was huge and powerful and determined to have his way with her. All too soon he had her plastered between the wall and the steel-hard muscles of his body.

Then his hard mouth was on hers, and his tongue inside her lips. Her breath caught in her throat as she began to ache for all of him and his lovemaking, but most especially his love. Remembering yesterday when their naked bodies had writhed, she moaned softly. He pulled away and laughed.

"Congratulations, *Mrs. Duke,*" he whispered, wiping off her kiss with the back of his brown hand.

"I'm sorry," she sobbed quietly. "Make love to me."

"After Uncle Duncan's had you, too? Sorry. Maybe he wants my seconds, but I don't want his."

"Oh... How dare—"

She couldn't deny what he accused her of, so she closed her eyes, too ashamed to look at him.

He shot her a final, sardonic glance. Then he turned on his heels and leaped down the ladder, his boots crashing on the slender rungs, taking them two at a time.

She sank to her knees in the prickly hay.

Her mouth burning from his kisses, "Tony," she cried. "I'm sorry...."

"You got what you wanted—the ranch. The house...Duke Ranch."

"No. I got what you wanted."

"Gold digger." His final word rang sharper than a slap.

"Tony, you have to let me explain. I don't care what the others think of me...not even Aunt Patty. But...I have to explain to you."

"What's to explain? You made love to me. Then you married a rich old man—who hates his own family—for his money. You stole him from your aunt. I don't know what I was ever thinking of to fall so crazy in love with the shallow likes of you."

"Crazy in love? Were you really crazy in love?"

"Not anymore—Aunt Zoe," he said with malicious tenderness.

She crawled to the edge of the loft and began to cry in earnest. In the past her tears had always softened him, but today they had the opposite effect.

"Congratulations!" he snarled.

Then the barn doors slammed together behind him.

He was gone, and she was alone in the dark. She heard his truck roar away, tires spitting white rocks and dust. She wrapped her arms around her waist and stayed where she was for a long time.

Then she touched her mouth with her trembling fingertips. She didn't hate him. No matter what he'd done or said, she never would. But that was only half her problem. She was married to the town's most disreputable citizen. It didn't matter that she had almost total amnesia about most of the wedding night and the ceremony.

The documents and photographs in her bedroom drawer were valid. The ring was real, too.

Slowly she climbed down from the loft and stumbled outside. She opened a gate and let herself into the closest pasture, which was ablaze with fluttering bluebonnets. The sun was hot pink against the distant horizon.

On impulse she peeled Duncan's big diamond off her slim finger. Her hand fisted around the hated gem. Closing her eyes, she spun round and round until she was so dizzy and breathless she could barely stand. Then she flung the ring as hard and as far as she could into the sea of flowers.

Trees whirled even after she opened her eyes. The earth beneath her feet felt uneasy. Hands outstretched, she groped at the air before slowly crumpling to the ground where she gagged and threw up.

She lay there in the thick blossoms for a long sickening interval before the will to live ebbed back into her body. Numbly she watched pink clouds float above her head and remembered lying on the ground like this, holding hands with Tony watching the clouds.

Tony… Ring or not, she was still married to the wrong man.

When it was dark, and she felt a little better, it became very important to find that ring. She stood up and began pacing the pasture methodically. Only, she couldn't find it.

She was married to the wrong man. She wanted out of this marriage, to give his ring back. Only she'd thrown the ring away.

But what did anything matter if Tony hated her?

What in the world was she going to do?

One

Nine years later

Anthony Duke felt so cold and alone that he shivered as the truck he drove hurtled through the high, wrought-iron gates of Memory Lane Cemetery.

"Slow down, son," his mother commanded.

"Hell." His boot tapped the brake.

Maybe he felt alone, but he wasn't. Henrietta Duke, his short, stout mother, who had an iron will, sat beside him, her gnarled fingers repeatedly rubbing circles around her kneecap. Noah, his hyper, eight-year-old son, was slumped in the back seat over one of his electronic games that made nerve-racking, beeping noises as he tapped the plastic keys.

Not that the illusion of solitude was strange to Anthony. He'd lived with it for years—when he'd been with Rene and Noah, as well as when he was out in some desolate pasture working cattle or in one of his breeding barns where he worked to improve deer stock to sell to other ranchers.

Something warm and bright had gone out of his life a helluva long time before Rene had died.

"Daddy! Do little boys ever get new mommies?"

Anthony hissed in a breath.

That same question again.

The lines around his mouth deepened. Rene had been dead a year. His ranch hands, his mother, and even his son were constantly pressuring to set him up with someone.

The cab of the pickup went deathly still. Was it that cemeteries seemed quieter than the rest of the world? Or was it just his guilty conscience? He had no right coming here.

"Do they get new mommies?"

Anthony's chest tightened. "We already had this conversation. No."

"What if you got married again? Would *she* be my new mommy?"

Anthony's fingers gripped the steering wheel as he headed toward Rene's grave. "We're here for your mother's birthday. You can't replace her. I'm not getting married again. Not in this lifetime. End of conversation."

But it wasn't. His mother, who was tuned in to him like radar, had her eye on him. Noah's questions and Anthony's answers lingered in the silence as Noah pressed his nose to the glass window to look at the orderly rows of tombstones.

"Why do people have to leave these junky artificial flowers and wreaths? Don't they know that they fade almost as soon as they put them out under fierce south Texas sun?'' his mother whispered.

''Because real flowers die.''

Anthony wished he hadn't said anything. When she turned to regard him, Anthony kept his eyes glued to the black asphalt. Still, he was aware of her fingers making those incessant circles on her knee.

''Well, except for the fake flowers, this place is one of the prettiest in the county,'' she exclaimed. ''Look at the trees! Except for the ebony and live oak, they've almost all lost their leaves,'' his mother continued.

Anthony gritted his teeth.

''The grass is mostly brown, but there's still quite a few patches of green,'' she continued, her fingers skimming her knee even faster.

''Do you think I'm blind? I can see trees and grass.''

The fingers froze on her kneecap. ''Edgy aren't we? You've been spending way too much time alone.''

''My life is none of your business.''

''What life? And don't tell me my son and my grandson are none of my business.''

Anthony slowed down as they neared the big gray tombstone that spelled out Duke.

''*D-U-K-E!* There she is!'' Noah cried.

Anthony shut the engine and opened his door, but the wind howled and slammed the heavy black door back in his face.

Guilt rushed through him. Who was he trying to fool with these visits to Rene's grave? He had no right to pretend grief for his perfect wife.

Well, he'd pretended for eight long years, hadn't

he? He and Rene had fooled everybody...except themselves. And except maybe his mother and Zoe's aunt Patty.

It was the first of February, yet this far south the afternoon was warm. The winter ice storm that gripped most of the United States had not reached south Texas. The temperature was in the eighties. He was wearing a white cotton shirt and a pair of old jeans. In another month, no telling how hot it would be. Or how cold.

"Looks like we've got the place to ourselves." Henrietta unsnapped her seat belt.

"Not many people make social calls to cemeteries," Anthony said.

"Shh," whispered Henrietta.

"Why is this necessary? There's nobody here."

"Mommy's here," Noah said quietly.

She's gone. Handle it. People die. Thousands, millions die, violently, peacefully or slowly and too young as Rene had. But the world keeps on turning. Time keeps passing.

People betray you in worse ways—they kill you and leave you alive.

Keeping his thoughts to himself, Anthony whirled around just as Noah stuffed his game into his sling pouch. The will to speak his mind died when he saw his son's grubby, little-boy hands with the black moons beneath the fingernails clutching a withered bunch of purple wine cups. How solemn his face had been as he'd knelt and picked them one by one, selecting the very best blossoms from the field in front of the house.

"How Rene loved flowers," Henrietta said.

"When do bluebonnets bloom, Dad?"

"March." Anthony bit out the word because bluebonnets always reminded him of someone he preferred never to think about.

"'Member how she liked bluebonnets, Dad?"

A vision of a girl in blue gingham, not Rene, never Rene, sitting in a field of bluebonnets rose in Anthony's mind. He fought against the image, tried to dutifully replace it with Rene—fought and failed—as always.

Old girlfriends? Was everybody haunted by old girlfriends?

"Can we pick some and take 'em to Mom in March?"

"Sure we can." Anthony threw his door open and jumped out of the cab before it could blow back on him again.

"Are you all right?" his mother whispered.

Anthony shrugged. It was a test of his nerves when Noah shot out behind him and skipped eagerly through the tombstones with his bouquet and thermos toward Rene's grave. It was as if the boy expected her to rise up and hug him.

Daddy! Do little boys ever get new mommies?

"Why the hell does he drag us here every damn week?"

"Shh," his mother said.

What if you got married again?

"Just go with him," Henrietta said. "I know it isn't easy, but that's all you have to do."

"When is he going to get over her?"

"When are you?"

Their black eyes met and locked. Then a fierce gust nearly blew off his Stetson. He grabbed the sweat-stained, cowboy hat and pitched it into the back seat. When his longish, black hair fell against his brow, he combed back the thick strands with his callused fingers.

Why wouldn't his mother stop looking at him? He hated the way he always felt as transparent as glass around her.

As soon as he removed his hand, his hair blew back into his eyes. "Damn."

"'Bout time for a haircut," Henrietta said as he loped around the hood to her side of the truck.

"Don't nag," he said as he opened her door and helped her out.

Dead leaves crunched under his boots as he began walking. Soon he stepped up behind Noah, who was pouring water out of his thermos into the urns on either side of the massive gray tombstone. Carefully Noah knelt and tried to arrange the pitiful-looking flowers in the urns. He hadn't picked enough, and the wind caught the fragile blossoms and sent them tumbling across the brown grasses onto other graves.

Noah's face went white and stark. His pupils seemed pinpricks of black in the middle of blazing blue irises. "Dad—"

Noah was chasing after the flowers. The wind had scattered them in all directions. Soon Noah was back, his eyes brighter, his lashes wet. He looked up at his father, but Anthony stared at the two shredded flowers with the broken stems.

"I couldn't catch them."

The boy had straight yellow hair and big eyes that burned Anthony. Why did he have to look exactly like his mother?

Anthony knelt and beckoned Noah closer.

Noah, who used to fly into his mother's arms, held on to the flowers and hung his head.

Anthony flushed, not knowing what to do or say. So, he read the dates etched in the gray polished stone beneath Rene's name. She was buried beside his father, Anthony Bond Field.

"Your father died young, too," Henrietta said. "You were only a year old when they brought him home."

"I don't remember him. You wouldn't talk about him. Why did you take your maiden name back?"

"Because he ran off after you were born. He wasn't much of a husband, and he certainly wasn't much of a father. But the name Duke meant a lot more around here than Field, so I took it back. I had to be a mother and a father to you," Henrietta continued, "just as you have to be both for Noah."

Anthony stared at the dates on his father's tombstone. Then his gaze drifted back to Rene's stone.

Dates? Was that all a life added up to in the end?

Rene was dead.

Noah backed away from him and ran to his grandmother. Slowly Anthony stood up.

He couldn't quit looking at those dates. Strange how he felt just as dead as she was. He closed his eyes and then covered them with his work-roughened palms. The wind rushed through the trees, battering his face, plastering his shirt against his broad chest. His hell went soul deep.

He stared at his mother who held his son.

When had it all gone wrong?

He knew when.

Again he saw *that* pixie face in the sea of bluebonnets. Not Rene's face. Never Rene's face. But a slim, young face with long-lashed, brown eyes and flyaway auburn hair, which she'd washed every day just so it would be shiny and soft for him. How he'd loved to wind that sweet-smelling silken mane through his fingers. Sometimes he'd used it to pull her close—the better to kiss her, to smell the lilacs in her shampoo, the better to love her.

Yes, he knew why. *She* was the reason he felt stripped of everything. He'd cheated Rene in so many ways…and all for a woman who'd betrayed him in the worst possible way.

He stared at his dead wife's tombstone. "What the hell can I do about any of it now, Rene? I'm thirty."

"Only thirty?" said his mother.

Anthony didn't realize he'd spoken aloud.

"You should start seeing new people," his mother said. She nodded toward Noah. "Make a life for him."

Noah, who looked thin and small, his golden hair spiking in the wind, was walking listlessly toward the truck.

"If you mean women…no way."

"You have to move on…for his sake," she said.

"You never remarried. I'll move on to dinner. But that's it. How about a steak?"

"You know you promised Noah we'd eat at Madame Woo's…."

"That damned Chinese restaurant again! A man could starve on the mountain of grass flavored with soy sauce they serve there."

"Shh…"

Rene had been on a constant diet to keep her perfect figure. Madame Woo's had been her favorite Chinese restaurant.

"Why can't he let her go?" Anthony asked.

"Why can't you?"

For a second the pixie face wreathed in a garland of bluebonnets flashed with ghostly brilliance in his imagination. A flush burned up his neck and scalded his cheeks. He flinched with guilt. He turned before his mother could read him. Then he ran with long, impatient strides, as if a dozen demons were chasing him instead of one slim ghost in blue gingham, toward the big black truck on the asphalt drive.

Anthony scowled. "Noah!" he shouted. "Time to go!"

"Next time, can we bring her bluebonnets?"

"Sure. Sure. Just get in."

On the way to the restaurant, his mother told Noah stories and tried to maintain a cheerful atmosphere. From time to time she would pause and wait for Anthony to add something. When he didn't, her voice grew even brighter and her manner more determined at merriment.

Noah sat in the back, as silent as stone, his face glued to the back window as they sped away from the cemetery.

When they got to Madame Woo's, Noah ran ahead of the hostess and claimed Rene's favorite booth in the corner beside the windows. As the three of them settled into the red leather seats, the hostess started to remove the fourth place setting.

"No!" Noah cried.

"Will someone else be joining you?"

Nobody said anything. Noah grabbed the silverware and chopsticks and began trying to rearrange them on the black table. "I...I can't remember where the fork goes...." Blue eyes lasered in on Anthony.

"It doesn't matter. There's no fourth person. Take them away." Anthony scooped everything to one side.

Noah burst into tears. Before Henrietta could loop her arms around the boy, he jumped out of the booth and ran to the fish tank.

"Of all the insensitive..." Henrietta began.

"Rene's dead. It's a fact. I'm sorry about it," Anthony said. "But I didn't cause it, and I don't know what I can do about it. It's been a year."

"Today would have been her thirtieth birthday."

A waitress with two nose rings, an eyebrow ring, lots of ear studs and bunches of red pigtails appeared at their table, with a notepad and a big, toothy smile. "Can I take your drink order?"

"Water. We're in a hurry. I'll order everything at once," Anthony muttered. "Mother always takes number eighty."

"The vegetarian dish plus bean curds?" The waitress smacked a wad of gum and wrote laboriously.

"Without MSG," said Henrietta. "No sugar."

The pink wad of gum popped. "It doesn't come with sugar."

"I'll take sweet and sour pork," Anthony said. "And chicken strips for my son." Snapping the large, red menu shut, he went after Noah.

Noah was in no mood to return to the table, but he did. Not that he would allow his grandmother to pull him close. Not that he would smile or join in the conversation. When the food came, he stared at his father from beneath his brows and picked out the broccoli and mushrooms sulkily.

"Broccoli is good for you," Henrietta said.

Noah wrinkled his nose.

Finally even Henrietta quit her attempts at conversation. They ate in gloomy silence until the waitress with all the piercings slapped the restaurant bill and three fortune cookies on the table.

When Anthony reached for the last neatly folded cookie, an errant gust rattled the blinds.

Henrietta cracked her cookie open and directed a sharp glance toward her son. "A single kind word will keep one warm for years."

"Something wonderful is going to happen to you," Noah read, crumpling his fortune. "Like a new mommy, Nana?"

"Not that again," Anthony muttered warningly.

Noah leaned closer to his grandmother. "Do fortunes come true?"

"Sometimes…if you believe really hard," she whispered.

Noah shut his eyes very tightly. Again the wind gusted through the screens and made the blinds rattle.

"Don't feed him that pap." Anthony tore his cookie apart. One glance at the typed message had Anthony sucking in a breath and wadding the ridiculous fortune into a miniature ball the size of an English pea.

"What'd it say, Dad?"

"Nothing."

He got up from the table as his mother noisily unwadded his fortune. Her voice followed him as he made his way to the cash register to pay the bill.

"Reunion with a shady lady sets off fireworks."

"What's a shady lady, Nana?"

A pixie face in a sea of bluebonnets sprang to Anthony's mind. His hand shook as he slid his wallet out of his back pocket. His mother was watching him with that dangerous gleam in her eye.

"Zoe!" she said brightly. "Zoe Duke. Your Aunt Zoe. She's Shady Lomas's one and only shady lady! Anthony, remember that reporter who called her that when the scandal broke and your cousins sued her. This is great!"

"Don't mention Zoe Creighton to me—"

"Zoe Duke. Same as ours. She's your great-aunt, Noah."

"She is nothing to him." Anthony strode back to the table and ripped the fortune out of his mother's fingers before she could read it aloud again. "Don't give me that know-it-all smile, Mother." Angrily he stuffed the strip of paper into his pocket.

"You two want a ride home?" he demanded when they didn't budge. "Or is this a sleep-over?"

Before they could answer him, Anthony slammed out of the restaurant faster than if he'd been shot out of a cannon.

"Who's Aunt Zoe, Nana? What's the matter with Daddy?"

"Long story." Henrietta's mind was racing. Logic dictated she should despise Zoe for marrying her illegitimate half brother, the family's black sheep and the owner of Duke Ranch and the family house. But what woman worth her salt was dictated solely by logic? Zoe had the ranch and the house, and Anthony was still carrying a torch for her. Zoe was sweet and malleable. With proper training, she might make a perfect daughter-in-law. Besides, what other way could they get the ranch back? And then there was Noah, who wanted a new mommy.

"I like stories," Noah said.

"This one may be a doozie." What if Anthony still loved Zoe? What if she loved him back? What if there was a way to right all the old wrongs? What if a clever, liberal-minded woman tackled the problem?

Henrietta patted Noah's golden head. "Now you run along after your father. And don't you dare let him drive off without me."

When the glass door closed behind her grandson, Henrietta pulled her cell phone out of her purse and punched in the number of Patty Creighton, her maddening best friend. Patty had been lording it over the whole town, especially her, ever since Duncan had died and made Zoe the richest woman in several counties, even after all the lawsuits and settlements.

When Zoe had run off to Manhattan to play editor, Patty had installed herself in the Duke ranch house and pretended she was its mistress. Patty was every bit as flashy, maybe more so than Uncle Duncan had ever been even at his worst. She bought herself a brand-new red Cadillac every year.

"Why are all of them red?" Henrietta had asked Patty once in a showroom.

"So people won't forget him."

Aunt Patty had a dozen furs locked up in her deep freeze. She even had a younger boyfriend.

Money! What it did to people!

As usual, Patty, who was a total couch potato, didn't answer the phone.

"Patty, pick up," Henrietta harped when the machine came on. "This is Henrietta. Quit playing computer bridge. Get off your plump tail and pick up."

Patty had put on a couple of pounds a year since

they'd been girls. Thirty plus years at two pounds a year added up.

"Hello!" The single word of Patty's greeting was followed by heavy breathing.

"What's your darling Zoe, our shady lady, up to these days?"

Patty was still trying to catch her breath. "Plump tail..."

"Maybe you should see a heart specialist—"

"Is this conversation going somewhere? Or are you just stirring your long nose in my business for the hell of it?"

"I asked you about Zoe."

"I was just going to call her and find out."

"She's still single, isn't she?"

"Last I heard. She says New York is no city to catch a man."

"I've got the most brilliant idea."

"Oh, dear! This sounds like trouble."

"With a capital *T.* It has to do with your niece and my stubborn son."

Patty caught her breath. "Shoot!"

Two

"Wow! You've got another bestseller!"

"I'm just the editor," Zoe whispered.

"Spare me." Ursula, the editorial director of Field and Curtis Publishing, was black and gorgeous. More than gorgeous. Even though she was in her late forties, she had the face and figure of a supermodel. Usually she was self-contained and serene, sailing through hectic days at the office without a trace of visible emotion.

Not today. Ursula was weeping and laughing as she read Veronica Holiday's manuscript. Veronica had that effect on readers. The book was very late, months overdue—as usual—but it was another winner.

Ursula, who was an old friend of Aunt Patty's from her Vassar days, had an impressive corner office with views of skyscrapers as well as a wedge of greenery in the hazy distance.

Someday, Zoe thought, her gaze skimming her boss's sleekly modern desk with its neatly piled manuscripts. Mentally she compared it to her own cluttered, windowless cubbyhole littered with notes to herself, unopened mail and dog-eared manuscripts—not to mention the posters of movie stars tacked all over her walls. A bookworm by nature and a frustrated writer, Zoe loved working with authors. It was all the rest of it—juggling her correspondence, the deadlines and the editorial meetings that stressed her. And she was an absolute failure when it came to the politics of her department. Why couldn't she have been born with a gene for organization?

Zoe hovered anxiously over her boss's shoulder. Ursula continued dabbing her eyes. "More tissue?"

Ursula flipped the last page, turned it over. Then she shuffled through the mailer to make sure she hadn't lost some pages. "Not again."

"I...I'm afraid..."

When Ursula's perfectly shaped black brows rose ever so slightly in her boldly classic face, Zoe's stomach did a somersault.

"What? What happens next?" Ursula asked.

To cover her fear Zoe took her time lowering her damp tissue from her brown eyes. Smoothing a wayward tangle of auburn that had escaped her ponytail, she bought a few more seconds to mull on her answer. "What? What happens, er, next?"

"That's right."

Zoe tried to look innocent or suave or whatever it was a working girl—correct that—a working *person* in publishing was supposed to look like. Correct that. *An editor.*

Her mind began to race. Yes, she was an editor! No. Not just an editor. An associate editor—and a rising star in her own right. And all because she had discovered Veronica Holiday. Only Veronica hadn't been a household name then. She'd been Juanita Lopez, a plain, plump nobody with a chip on her shoulder. No, make those twin boulders on both her shoulders.

Zoe had discovered her in the slush pile…when she should have been at an editorial meeting.

Nobody would ever forget that day at Field and Curtis. Ursula had sent her secretary after her. Zoe had been on the floor of her office, pages everywhere, reading this weird, wonderful novel, *Bad Boyfriends.*

The novel, which was about a married woman who couldn't get over her old bad-boy boyfriend, had held Zoe spellbound. Apparently, the old boyfriend hadn't been able to forget about the woman either because he was stalking her. As usual, Veronica had sent that first book in without an ending. Only Zoe had known how it had to end. And she'd called her. The resulting book had been that year's sensation. Since then every Veronica Holiday book had done better than the last one.

The trouble was, Zoe's claim to fame, her job, her career, *everything* depended on Veronica, and if Veronica was anything, besides being famous, talented and highly neurotic, it was in a word—undependable. Oh! And superdifficult.

Take her hair. It was a different color every time she made one of her surprise trips to New York. Last night it had been orange. And spiky. And her weight. Six months ago she'd been a blimp in flowing, big-flowered gowns. Back then she'd hidden beneath big hats that had made her look even heavier.

Last night she'd been a Titian-haired wraith in a skimpy, see-through blouse and skintight, snakeskin pants. She'd had a slim, new nose that made her ever so much prettier.

"What went with the silky blond curls?" Zoe had asked while they'd sat in oversize highback velvet chairs. She and Veronica had munched figs from Venetian goblets bigger than their heads at the famous restaurant Veronica had demanded Zoe take her to.

"Blond curls weren't me."

"I can see that."

"Where's the rest of it?" Ursula now repeated, her silken tone barely concealing a steely edge of impatience.

Three police cars shot beneath Ursula's office, screaming toward the park in the midmorning gray light. Velvet chairs, gleaming gilt, mahogany wainscoting, orange hair and the slim, new nose dissolved. Zoe realized her mind had been a million miles away.

"What happens next?" Ursula whirled around in her chair, and stared at her.

Zoe had asked Veronica the same question last night. And Veronica had wailed. "We'll...we're...I mean Veronica's on top of that," Zoe said.

"She's really painted herself into a corner this time."

"That's what makes her books so great," Zoe murmured defensively. "Her characters are all so vulnerable and impulsive, and they get themselves into the most impossible jams."

"The plots are as wild as her characters. The barge that contains enough toxins to destroy the ocean is breaking apart in a storm. The hero has been stabbed and is locked in the bowels of the ship. The bad guy, who's a sex fiend, has the girl and their baby. The hero..."

"When Czar went after him with a meat hook, I nearly died."

Zoe had always had an overactive imagination. She loved stories and had a headful of fantasies. In fact, she still had fantasies about a certain cowboy from her own past.

"Don't think about him," said a silent voice in Zoe's head. "You're doing it, anyway," said another.

Ursula ran long slim fingers through her sleek cap of straight black hair. "What are you doing here?"

"This is my job. I work here."

"Get to the Plaza Athenee. Get Veronica up. Get her writing."

"But she has her heart set on lunch at the Russian Tea Room. She's got a new gold outfit that matches the decor."

"Does she do anything but eat and sleep and shop for outrageous clothes?"

"Men. Since she got skinny and pretty, she's started chasing men. She's a walking disaster when it comes to men."

"When?"

"When what?" Zoe asked.

"Knock. Knock." Ursula rapped her desk.

"Hello. Lunch? Russian Tea Room? Bestseller with no ending?"

"Twelve-thirty."

When Ursula's dark-chocolate eyes fell to her designer wristwatch, she gasped. "You're late. As always. Find her! You're her muse! Get her writing! Now!"

"Two o'clock. No! Ten minutes past two!"

The snooty waiter in elegant black with a nose as long as a suicidal ski jump, was getting surlier by the second. He must've asked Zoe a dozen times if she wanted to order.

Zoe's stomach grumbled. "Veronica, where are you?"

When two stylish ladies at the next table turned and stared at her, Zoe cupped her hands over her mouth. Bad habit—talking to yourself. Besides that, Zoe was underdressed in a black skirt and rumpled sweater. She didn't ooze old money or new money, either, like most of the other diners did. "I'm on an expense account," she said under her breath. "A very large expense account."

Instead of reading the menu again, which she'd already memorized, Zoe's gaze flitted from the door to her own pale, disheveled reflection in the mirrored walls. Masses of auburn hair framed her stark white oval face.

She looked anxious. She was alone. In a word—she was pathetic.

"Girl, don't you know that big hair is a no-no in New York." She fluffed the unruly stuff. "I should cut it."

As always the other voice inside her head talked

back. Did everybody have voices in their heads? Or just frustrated writers who became editors?

"You've been telling yourself that, ever since you got here six years ago."

"Vanity. That's what's stopping me. I'm a Southern girl at heart. Why, every little-town Texas girl knows that big hair is power. Power over..."

Unbidden came the memory of Tony's hands in her hair.

Tony. Why couldn't she get over him? What was it with these fantasies about Tony?

Did women ever get over their old boyfriends? Or were youthful loves part of a woman's unique personal myth and mystery? Maybe Zoe identified with Veronica's work because she and Veronica shared an incredible vulnerability, an impulsiveness that got them into all kinds of trouble and into these disturbing fantasies about their old boyfriends.

Tony had loved her long hair. Loved to play with it and kiss it. Loved to watch it blow in the warm, south-Texas spring winds. She'd lain on top of him in the loft, and he'd wrapped it around his throat and made her feel like a goddess. Nobody in Manhattan had ever made her feel so adored.

It had been nine years since Tony.

"This is bad! Don't think about him!"

"But he's the reason I ran away after college and stayed gone. Not the scandal."

After Duncan's death and the vicious legal battles with his daughters over his inheritance, Zoe had finished college. Upon graduation, she'd wanted to get far away from Sandy Lomas and from Anthony and Rene and their new baby, from everybody in south

Texas who thought she was evil because she'd married the rich old reprobate.

Was it her fault Duncan had had a heart attack when she'd told him she'd lost his ring and wanted a divorce or an annulment? Apparently, a week before their marriage, Duncan had learned he had a huge, inoperable aneurysm. He'd confessed to her, "I decided if I was going to die, I want to go out with a bang! You're the bang!"

Duncan had pulled through that first crisis, only to get into a royal fight with both his daughters in the hospital over his marriage.

"She's got to be thirty years younger than you are," they'd screamed.

"Please—I'm a dying man."

Indeed, tubes were snaking from dozens of gurgling machines to various parts of his body. Bags of drugs were dripping into his thin arm.

"She's after your money, you old fool."

"Oh, is she?" he'd pulled Zoe closer, and dozens of red lights began to flash on his monitor. "Then I'd best give her what she wants, hadn't I?"

They should have known how perverse he was. First thing, he'd changed his will and left Zoe everything. Then he'd sent his girls and Anthony and Henrietta copies of the will just to stir them up. The girls had gotten so hopping mad, they'd accosted him again, this time on the main steps of the Methodist Church. He'd grabbed his heart and had a second attack and died in Zoe's arms on the spot.

His last words to Zoe as she'd knelt over him on those concrete steps had been, "I don't care what it costs, don't let them have a dime. They murdered me. Oh, and finish college.... Don't let our crazy marriage stop you from finish—" He'd gasped, and his eyelids had fluttered. He'd smiled and was gone.

"Somebody help him! Please," Zoe had screamed.

Suddenly Anthony had knelt beside her. She'd caught his clean, male scent and had realized how everything about him had haunted her.

"I'm afraid he's gone," he'd said.

"It's my fault."

He'd cupped her chin and lifted it so that she was forced to meet his blazing eyes. "No," he'd said gently, surprising her. "He was just a very sick man."

"Oh, Anthony..."

Rene had called to him then. He'd gotten up and taken her hand.

"See you around, Zoe," Rene had said.

Of course Zoe had settled with his daughters, and the girls had gotten way more than a few dimes. But that hadn't stopped them from gossiping all over town about Zoe Duke being a gold digger. The talk was still so fierce Zoe couldn't go home without people turning their heads and treating her as if she was a scarlet woman.

But it was the sightings of a certain tall, dark cowboy and his darling little son that drove her back to New York with the fresh determination to show the world—to show him—she didn't need anybody's money.

She could make it on her own. She *had* made it.

Liar. She was still running from Tony. She couldn't forget the last time she'd seen him. He'd been smiling tenderly down at Rene in church. Rene had been so sick and thin, but her smile for her husband had made her radiant. How sad he'd looked then, how utterly devastated. How much he must've loved Rene, his perfect wife. And, oh, how lost and abandoned and petty and small Zoe had felt watching them.

Because of him, she'd come to New York broken-hearted, disillusioned but determined to make it big in this tough, tough city. Anthony was the one she had to prove herself to. She was still trying to show *him,* drat his hide. And she would. She would!

He'd had the perfect marriage to the beautiful, perfect Rene, who'd given birth to the perfect son. Now that Rene was dead, he couldn't get over her. Aunt Patty talked about him more than ever, telling Zoe about his weekly visits with his little boy to the cemetery.

"He always takes wildflowers. His heart is in the grave. He says he'll never marry—"

"I'm sorry for him, but please, don't tell me about him!"

"His little boy— He's a bright little monkey. A lot like Rene. He needs a mother."

"Don't."

"What about you? When are you going to get married?" Aunt Patty had asked slyly.

"Been there. Done that. Remember?"

"I am talking about a real marriage."

"I know you mean well, but that question is extremely annoying. Surely you've got something better to do than to meddle in my life, which is something you don't know anything about, Aunt Patty."

"Do you have a boyfriend?"

"Abdul."

"What kind of name is that?"

"His last name's Izzar. He's from Iraq."

"Oh. Don't guys like that have harems?"

"Abdul is an American citizen now."

"Abdul Izzar. Well, I wouldn't tell the folks here about him, honey."

"He's a commodities trader. Very smart."

"Why don't you come home to Texas where you belong?"

"Because I came to this city with a big dream."

"One you have yet to realize."

"Oh, Aunt Patty..."

"What's wrong with getting married and having babies?"

"We are living on an overpopulated planet."

"You just think that because you live in New York and read too much."

Zoe wasn't sure she'd accomplished anything in the years she'd lived in Manhattan other than fall on her face about ten thousand times. New York had a way of gobbling the unwary whole. At night sometimes she woke up feeling lost and all alone, her head spinning with dreams about Tony.

Her dream was always the same. At first, she was in the dark. It was misty, and she was all alone and trembling with fear. Then she felt someone there and the mist parted. Tony's brown hand was reaching for her, pulling her close. She wanted him so much and she could see the desire in his eyes. But she always woke up before they made love. Then she would lie awake—aching.

Nine years. How long did it take to get over somebody who hadn't even let her explain, who'd gone on with his own life as if he'd never much cared about her in the first place?

When she'd been unable to land a job in Manhattan on her own, Aunt Patty had called her old friend, Ursula, told her Zoe was a bookworm who had several unpublished novels in her attic, and Ursula had set up an interview.

Zoe was fiddling with her silverware and staring blankly at an enormous golden tree dripping with lighted eggs when her cell phone rang.

"It's me-e-e," Veronica drawled, her north Texas voice as whiny and twangy as a loose guitar string. Only last night she'd confided she was taking voice lessons to eliminate the accent. She didn't apologize for being late, Zoe noted. Bad sign.

"I can't do lunch," Veronica blurted. "I don't even know if I can live until tomorrow."

"Oh, dear."

"I pigged out at this deli, too. Three bagels. Cheese. Croissants, too. A cream puff even—"

"Croissants!"

"Oozing with butter and raspberry jam. Sugar! I ate sugar!"

Zoe's stomach rumbled. "This is bad. Where are you? I'll come...."

"I got on the Web."

Oh, dear. "I told you never to do that again."

"I...I was going to write. I felt a glimmer...you know, like the story was beckoning me. So, I turned on my laptop."

"This is good."

"But..."

"But..." Zoe hung on the word.

"Some bitch wrote *Lovers Don't Tell* stinks." Veronica burst into tears.

"*Lovers* made number one on every single list that

matters! There are lots of crazy, jealous people out there who need to get a life. Unfortunately, they all have keyboards and write nasty critiques.''

''She killed me.''

''Look, just come to lunch.''

''Food? Now? I can barely snap the waistband of my gold mini. My black mesh panty hose keep sliding under my belly the way they used to when I was so fat. I'm going for a walk in the park.''

''This is good. You're going for a walk in the park in a gold mini and black mesh stockings. I…I'll meet you.''

''I'm too suicidal for company.''

''Which is why—''

Veronica hung up.

Zoe stared at her cell phone. It was all she could do not to pound it on the table.

''Excuse me, madam—'' The snooty waiter stared down his impressive nose at Zoe's big hair and frumpy black sweater.

''I'm not a member of an alien species,'' she said tartly.

''Would you like to order, madam?''

''Check, please,'' Zoe retorted.

West of midtown, Chelsea, the heart of the garment district, Zoe's neighborhood, was like a lot of young, affluent areas in Manhattan. Only, lots of the attractive couples walking together in front of the nineteenth-century town houses, holding hands, were men.

It was late. The sun had disappeared behind the town houses, and the streets and sidewalks were engulfed in shadows. Zoe felt harassed, stressed and even more ineffectual than usual as she hurried past the Flatiron building toward home.

The day had gone from bad to worse. She'd walked in the park for an hour looking for Veronica.

No gold mini or black mesh hose. So Zoe had gone back to the office.

Ursula had caught her in the copying room. "So, how's the book?"

"She's working on it."

No sooner had Ursula walked out than Zoe had felt so guilty about her lie that she had put the manuscript in wrong and jammed the last antiquated copy machine that had still been working. All the other editors had snapped at her because everybody had deadlines and couldn't copy anything.

Every time her phone rang, Zoe had jumped. But Veronica hadn't called. Finally, Zoe had left work early and was headed home on the hope that Veronica might get bored with her own company and turn up on her doorstep.

The sidewalks were jammed as she walked past people pushing garment racks. She knew the rules. Keep to the right. Walk fast. No eye contact.

This city. So many people racing places. Were any of them like her, going nowhere? Faking it when they weren't fantasizing about old boyfriends and old loves?

"We're like ants spinning, going nowhere on this tiny mudball."

"Veronica, where are you?"

"Don't talk to yourself. Don't talk to yourself."

"You're doing it. You're doing it."

Ed and Gujarat, the guys who lived in the apartment below hers, came out of Zoe's brownstone town house, holding hands. They lived on the fourth floor. Sometimes they carried her groceries up and then stayed and drank wine with her on her balcony.

Ed raised his eyebrows and looked surprised to see her. Gujarat nodded slyly.

"Hey, guys," she said smiling.

"By the sound of that banging upstairs, we thought you were home already," Gujarat said.

"We were happy for you." Ed worked his brow again.

She stopped at her mailbox and then ran up the stairs without giving their remarks nearly enough thought. She was always doing that—missing clues any idiot would have picked up on and then catching them later.

She was only slightly out of breath by the time she'd climbed the stairs to her front door. The forty-block walk from her office kept her in pretty good shape.

"Patience," she whispered as she fumbled in her purse. It always took her a while to find her key in the scramble of dollar bills, credit card receipts and lipstick cases.

Finally she found it and opened the door. Abdul's computer monitor with all the little numbers that flashed constantly across the screen was on.

Abdul. Right! She stomped the floor. Her hands fisted on the straps of her purse. Then she flung it onto the couch. She'd promised to cook steak and make a salad. He was coming to dinner. Oh, dear. She'd forgotten again.

They didn't live together, but he'd installed the monitor so that when he was there, he could watch it out of the corner of his eye.

Well, she couldn't cook. Not tonight. They'd have to do deli.

"Super Cat! Kitty, kitty, kitty..."

Usually her big fat tiger-striped baby came running to meet her. Zoe stepped inside the kitchen, picked up a can of gourmet cat food and slid it under her electric can opener. When the opener buzzed, and the lid popped open, she blew tuna fumes and called him again.

"Tuna, your favorite. Super Cat! Where are you, sweetie?"

Genuinely worried when he didn't come, she dumped the tuna into Super Cat's bowl and stepped into the hall. When her toe snagged on something, she looked down. Gold fabric littered the hallway. She knelt and picked up a gold, uplift bra. A man's dark-blue tie and black mesh panty hose were tangled in the golden bra straps. Zoe fingered the soft blue tie and nearly strangled on her next breath.

"I know you. I picked you out at Macy's and gave you to Abdul. I looped you around his neck last Christmas."

"Stop talking to yourself."

She looked up. Clothes seemed to have exploded off bodies in her hallway. Her eyes followed a trail of slinky gold and the rest of Abdul's clothing—his dress shirt, two black socks, only one black shoe—to her bedroom door.

She didn't realize her headboard had been slamming rhythmically against the wall, until the banging stopped.

"Oh...oh...oh..." A woman was panting in the bedroom.

Then Zoe saw the gold mini.

Oh, dear. This was bad.

Mentally Zoe counted the months since she'd last had sex. And that hadn't been rambunctious, headboard-banging sex. Or meaningful sex. Or anything at all, really. Since then, she and Abdul had just gotten interested in other things. Funny, she hadn't even thought about sex—except when she woke up dreaming about Anthony—until now.

"Meow!" A striped, brown paw reached out from under the hall closet door and snagged her ankle. A claw sank into her flesh. Blood spurted.

"Sweetie!" In a daze, she opened the closet door, and a roly-poly blob of brown and gold fur with flattened ears brushed past her into the kitchen. Super Cat was frantic for his bowl of tuna.

The bedroom door cracked, and Abdul stuck his black head out. "*Habeebti,* you're home early."

Zoe's tongue hit the tip of her front teeth and stuck there. Her throat froze. She tried to say something, but somehow she was so upset, all she could do was mouth soundless gulps of air.

Then she exchanged a wild, panicked glance with Super Cat before the cat wisely hunkered down to lick at his tuna.

Without a glance toward Abdul, Zoe sucked in an indignant breath. Then she whipped the clothes off the floor, went to her kitchen window and threw them out onto the street.

"*Habeebti!* What are you doing?" Abdul yelled.

"Don't you dare *habeebti* me!" He'd taught her that *habeebti* meant darling in Arabic. When pedestrians looked up, she waved his jockey shorts at them.

"Not my jockey shorts!" Abdul shrieked.

She dropped them and turned to smile brightly as Abdul, who, wearing only a towel, stomped barefoot into her kitchen.

"Out!" she purred, turning on him.

"This woman with red hair came here. Said she was looking for you. She attacked me."

"And you surrendered. Out!"

Green eyes slitted, Super Cat stopped eating tuna and glared at him for good measure.

"You locked Sweetie Baby in the closet."

"I can't believe I did that."

Zoe went to her front door and opened it for him. "I can't, either. If you don't go, there's going to be blood."

He scooted past her out into the hall. "You sure about this?"

She went over to the table, ripped the plug out of the wall, and carried his monitor to him.

"Take your monitor thingy." She rammed it into his hands.

"This city. What it does to people."

"Not this city—you. And her. It's been a crazy day—even for me!"

In a flash of impulsive brilliance, she yanked her towel from his waist, took a final glance at his sleek brown body that had reminded her of Anthony's and slammed the door in his startled face.

"Be honest. You only dated him because he sort of looks like Tony."

"Liar."

"Hush. You're doing it again. Hush."

Abdul banged on the door and screamed, "You'll be sorry!"

"No. I won't. You don't even read."

"What? I can't stand here naked and scream through your thick door."

"Then go get your jockey shorts. They're out on the street." She shot her dead bolt. "You tricked me. You read book reviews. You don't know anything."

"I know how to make money!"

"The less said at such times the better. Just go home." She stomped down her hall and yelled, "Veronica!"

No answer.

When Zoe opened her bedroom door, Veronica, clad only in bedsheets, was curled up like a sex kitten, scribbling frantically on a yellow legal pad she'd stolen from Zoe's desk.

"I was writing on that tablet."

"Go away," Veronica whispered desperately. "I've got it! Eureka! I've got the ending! Wow, you were wonderful when you came home! All that passion! You're gonna love my ending!"

"No, I won't. Because you're not going to write it! I'm going to part that orange mop of yours with…with…"

A big black umbrella stood in her corner. Zoe grabbed it and stalked toward Veronica. "With this umbrella."

Veronica leaped out of bed, trailing sheets and the lavender bedspread. "You're sore about Abdul?" Veronica was scrambling to pull her train of sheets through the bathroom door. "That dud, who can't talk about anything but positions in deutsche marks and Swiss francs…even in bed—I did you a huge favor."

They stared at each other.

"Huge," Veronica repeated.

She had a point.

Not that this was any time to concede high moral ground to the *other woman.* Still, Zoe dropped her umbrella an inch or two. Slowly she stepped out into her hall, closed the door and sagged against it.

"I'm a failure in every department. As a writer. As an editor. As a woman. As a New Yorker."

"Oh, and don't forget, you still have fantasies about your old boyfriend."

"You're doing it again."

"Shut up."

"I can talk to myself if I want to."

Zoe's kitchen phone began to ring.

Still muttering to herself, she walked back down the hall.

"How's single life in New York?" croaked Aunt Patty.

"Bad question," Zoe admitted.

"Bad timing?"

"Don't gloat."

"Who me?" A thoughtful pause. "How's Abdul?"

"He's history."

Aunt Patty emitted what sounded like a sigh of pure bliss. "Why, this is great timing. You sound as miserable as Tony."

"Tony's miserable?" The thought was too dangerously comforting.

"Why, Henrietta was telling me just yesterday," Aunt Patty continued.

"Stop right there! I'll hang up if you talk about him. He and I are not, hear this, we are not orbiting the same sun anymore."

"He's single. You're single. You're both miserable."

"Reality check. We broke up nine years ago. He lives in Texas. I live in New York."

"One of you has to make the first move."

"Not me—"

I still dream about him. I never date anybody who doesn't look like him.

"Aunt Patty—"

Neither of them said anything for a long moment. Twisting the phone cord, Zoe sank to the floor. "What's wrong with me, Aunt Patty? I messed everything up with Tony. I married Duncan to get even. Duncan married me for a lot of harebrained reasons, too. I was so stupid. Stupid. Stupid. And ever since…I haven't gotten one bit smarter. Why can't I do anything right?"

"It's not too late to start over."

"You got me this job. But I'm no good at it."

"Ursula loves you."

"I never meet my deadlines. I turn all my authors into prima donnas. I can't file. She's always telling me I can't prioritize. I…I can't say what I really think in editorial meetings.… Oh, and I break all the machinery."

"But you discovered that…that—"

"That monster!"

"How can you call her that? I've read all her books! Her characters are as crazy as all the people I know. And she dedicates all her books to you!"

"Let's not talk about her! I'm quitting. I'm leaving New York for good."

"Great. You can come home."

"Who was I kidding? I can't make it here. I can't

make it anywhere. If I didn't have Duncan's money, I'd be worse off than those homeless people sleeping in cardboard boxes in the park."

"Just come home."

She thought about Tony, about her crazy dreams. She'd never get over him if she went home. "I have to forget Tony."

"Why?"

"I can't come home, and that's final."

Another long, pensive silence.

Aunt Patty's voice was different, cautious. "Maybe, then, maybe you just need a little vacation. I could give you a week of my time share... anywhere in the world. I've already got a week traded for Greece."

"Greece?"

"Henrietta and I traded our time-shares for a week next month. And now we can't go...." Her voice trailed off.

Aunt Patty sounded a little funny, but Zoe didn't really pay attention.

"No way am I going to Greece."

"I'll fax you the brochure."

"I love the ending!" Ursula cried, elated. "Yes!" She made a fist and punched the air above her head. "Yes."

"Good. Maybe you can be her editor from now on." Zoe leaned across her desk and laid a rather wordy letter of resignation in front of her boss.

Ursula got halfway through the first paragraph and tore it in two.

"You can't quit. I won't let you."

"I am a complete failure. I've failed at everything."

"You're Veronica's muse."

"No."

"She said she was sorry. She sent you bushels of roses."

"She's too crazy for me."

"Her endings make her crazy. They make us all crazy. Take a month off. Go to Greece. You've earned a vacation."

"Did you talk to Aunt Patty?"

"She called me last night. She's very worried about you. Go to Greece. The time-share in Rhodes sounds wonderful. Think about your life. Figure out what you want to do with it. Don't throw your career as an editor away just on an impulse."

"Impulse?"

"That's your weakness. You're always leaping before you look…like Veronica's characters. You married Duncan.… Go to Greece."

"Greece? Why Greece? What's in Greece?"

"Your future. Trust me." But Ursula wouldn't meet her eyes.

Again, some instinct warned Zoe that Aunt Patty had told Ursula more than she was telling her, that Greece was somehow dangerous.

"Why Greece? What's in Greece?"

"Maybe the man of your dreams," Ursula replied.

Three

"Athens. Why can't I get excited about Athens, city of dust, bougainvillea, roses and short, boxy buildings?" Zoe wondered as her bus rolled through dry, red hills out to the airport on the edge of the city.

"This is the capital of Greece. You'd think somebody would think to build at least one hotel by the airport?"

"Hello? I had to take a bus into the center of town to find lodgings, an hour-long ride through thick traffic. I want Manhattan. Chelsea. Super Cat. And somebody besides me to talk to."

In a word, her vacation hadn't even begun, and she was already homesick and sick of her own company.

The bus she'd caught this morning at Syntagma Square in the heart of Athens rolled to a final stop.

Zoe, who was at the front of the bus, grabbed her backpack, leaped off and headed inside the terminal.

With difficulty she read the Greek signs. This country was like a perpetual eye exam. Traveling by herself was no fun, either. She felt so alone, so cut off and so dangerously vulnerable somehow. But at least most of the men left her alone. Greece reminded her of Mexico, only it felt safer. Still, it was a long way from Manhattan and everything that was familiar.

"Being alone is the whole point," Aunt Patty had said yesterday when she had called to wish Zoe a safe journey. "You'll have time to think. About your future."

"You never go anywhere by yourself. You always go with Henrietta Duke," Zoe had replied.

"Who never shuts up and refuses to play games with me."

"Wasn't she going to Rhodes with you? How come you two canceled?"

Aunt Patty had coughed nervously, mentioned doctors and changed the subject rather quickly. Which seemed odd now that Zoe thought about it. Yesterday Zoe had been in such a hurry to finish all her last-minute chores so she could make her plane. Why hadn't she paid more attention to Aunt Patty's evasive nonanswers?

Henrietta owned a time-share, and usually the two of them traded for the same week in the same locale. Zoe should have asked about her aunt's little cough. Had the two of them had a fight? Would Henrietta be in her time-share?

When Zoe got to the gate for her flight to Rhodes, she was three hours early and spacey from jet lag.

She sank down into a plastic chair and pulled out a paperback novel. The words blurred.

Even after a restful night's sleep in a small hotel in the Plaka with views of the Acropolis, she still felt strange and disoriented. It was weird to step on a plane in the U.S and get off in a foreign country. It was like some vital piece of herself hadn't arrived. It was probably 2:00 a.m. back in New York. Super Cat would be curled up on her pillow waiting for her to come to bed.

What was she doing here? Zoe hadn't had one coherent thought about her life on the endless flights to get here. Or her future.

If you ignored the columns and all those glorious naked male statues and the olive trees, Athens reminded her of west Texas. Dry, red dirt. West Texas had never been her favorite locale.

Her Greek hotel had been tinier and stuffier than a roadside motel in west Texas, too. She'd had to put her key in a slot in the wall just to turn on the electricity.

She opened her book and was soon lost in the story. She didn't look up until it was almost time for her flight and the lounge was filled with people.

Thinking she'd better go to the ladies' room, she slid her book into her purse. Then she got up and rushed down a wide hall. She was heading for a sign with a little fat lady above the door, when a small boy with straight yellow hair and loose shoelaces streaked out of the men's room and slammed into her so hard she almost fell on top of him.

"Oops," she said gently.

He'd been juggling a video game and sling pouch filled with little stuffed animals in one hand and a cola cup in the other. She caught the video game just as his soda sprayed all over her black skirt.

"Sorry," he whispered.

She helped him to his feet. "Careful." She handed his electronic game to him. "Are you okay?" she quizzed softly.

He was beet red. When he was done stuffing his game into his sling pouch, he stared up at her, his blue eyes desperately intense. "I've lost my daddy."

He rubbed at his eyes, and for a minute she was afraid he might cry. So she took his hand and pressed it reassuringly. "It's okay. I promise."

He gulped in a big breath of air, and she nodded.

He had thick straight yellow bangs, slim pointy ears, freckles and a gap between his two front teeth, which seemed huge compared to his baby teeth.

"We'll find him," she said.

She was about to stand up when a pair of long, black pointy-toed cowboy boots planted themselves on either side of the boy.

On either side of her, too.

Before she had time to look up, an all-too-familiar voice made her shiver. "There you are you little rascal! Damn it. I've been looking everywhere—"

"Do not cuss. He's just a little boy," Zoe said.

"My little boy! My son, damn it!"

Instantly the boy's blue eyes brimmed with tears.

"Oh, dear. I really do know that voice." She gasped as her eyes ran upward from his boots, up his long legs, up, up, up to his grim, dark, chiseled face.

Recognizing her old boyfriend instantly, she froze. *"Tony!"* Then the thought came, *Aunt P! You witch!*

Zoe's heart thudded wildly as she stood up to confront Anthony Duke. "Oh, dear. Oh, dear," she murmured to herself.

He cocked his head to one side. His brows arched.

"Hello, Tony," she whispered in the chilliest tone she could manage.

In that long moment before he spoke, the seconds ticked by one by one, as slowly as hours.

A jet rumbled down the runway. The floor beneath her shuddered. A blush heated her cheeks.

"*Zoe Duke?* Aunt Zoe?" he mocked.

"Oh, dear."

"What in the hell are you doing here?" he demanded.

"I asked you not to cuss in front of your son."

"I want an answer." His cold black gaze filled her with dread. "Don't bother. I can guess." He gave her a slow, insinuating appraisal. "Of all the low-down, sneaky…"

"Wh-what are you doing in Athens?" she stammered.

Had he always been so huge? So intimidating?

No. He'd been tall, but he'd been more boy than man. Now he was filled out. He was a big man, whose broad shoulders were heavily muscled from real work on the range and not from some expensive, Manhattan gym. He was dark from the sun and long hours in the saddle. His large brown hands were rough.

Oh, dear. And he was handsome. Too handsome. Her pulse was racing just because he was standing so close. She hated the way she was overreacting to him.

"I fell down, Daddy," the boy said. "I hurt my knee."

When Tony knelt, his large, masculine, brown hands ran gently over the boy's legs to make sure he was all right. Just watching those hands made the world slow down and other conversations die away.

Old boyfriends. She was always buying novels that had to do with old boyfriends.

The little boy, Rene's son, was staring up at her. His big eyes blazed as startlingly blue as Texas bluebonnets, just like Rene's used to, and yet he looked so vulnerable.

"Rene," Zoe murmured. How sad it must have been for her to get sick and know she had to leave such a beautiful little boy.

He was wearing a torn beige T-shirt and long, wrinkled shorts. All his clothes were too big. His athletic shoes were too big, too. He needed a mother to dress him, a mother to cut his hair, to make him wash his hands, to tie his shoes, to scrub his fingernails.

"You know my mommy, too?" The little boy looked up at her, his intense eyes bewildered.

"You...must be Noah—" Zoe tried to look anywhere but at Tony and his darling son.

"Should he call you Auntie Zoe?" Tony drawled in a cocky tone that set her on edge. "Technically, he's your great-nephew and I'm...I'm your nephew."

"By marriage!" she exhaled the word.

"Yes. *By marriage.*"

She felt a wealth of regrets.

"So, what are you doing here, Zoe? When my mother talked me into this trip, I should have suspected a trick," Tony accused.

"Me?" She stiffened. "I'm the one who's been

scammed. Ever since Rene died, Aunt P can't stop talking about you."

"Any more than my busybody mother can stop talking about you," he murmured, his deep voice softening in some subtle manner that was highly disturbing. And did he have to rake her body with those hooded black eyes of his?

"Wh-why can't they accept the fact that we hate each other?" she asked.

"Apparently they never got over us breaking up." His gaze lingered on her swelling bosom beneath her dark sweater.

"I would have forgotten you years ago if...if..."

"So, you haven't forgotten me," he mused dryly.

"How could I, er, when...when Aunt Patty brings you up constantly. But that's beside the point. I didn't plan this. They're a pair of stubborn, meddlesome old fools."

"Is this lady really my aunt, Dad?"

"She's just someone I used to know," Tony muttered.

"Just someone?" Zoe groaned. *I was a virgin, you jerk.* "Just someone? That's rich."

"Did you know my mommy?" Noah persisted.

"She was my best friend." Zoe studied the beautiful boy with new wonder.

"So, have I heard of you?"

"Probably not. She and I were friends a long time ago."

"Nine years ago," Tony said in that voice that chilled her.

"I'm eight." Noah whirled around, holding up eight fingers.

"See. Ancient history. Before you were born."

Zoe ruffled his hair affectionately. The boy moved closer to her as if he craved being touched by a woman's loving hand.

''So, what are we going to do about this?'' Tony demanded of Zoe.

''What do you mean?''

''This disaster? Who's not going to Rhodes?''

''I didn't lose two nights of sleep, fly all the way over here just to fly all the way back to Manhattan.''

''Neither the hell did we.''

''So—''

''Why can't we all go, Dad?'' Noah whispered in a small, shy voice.

Tony glared at her until Zoe blushed. His eyes were so piercing she began to wonder if her sweater and skirt had suddenly become transparent. Was he assessing changes in her physical appearance as swiftly as she was assessing them in him?

He was taut, tall and lethally magnificent. His carved face had a few more lines, especially around his mouth and eyes. He was huge, and he exuded male virility and anger—lots of anger, all of it directed at her.

His black eyes blazed. Well, at least she had his full attention. She remembered how jealous she used to be of him. She'd been so insecure. So young.

It bothered her to realize that she'd measured every boyfriend to Tony, and none of them had come close.

''Can we sit by her, Dad?''

''What?'' Tony growled.

''No!'' she whispered, just as frantic as Tony.

''On the plane?'' Noah queried insistently.

''No,'' both adults chimed.

"But you don't talk to me, Dad. And you won't play games—"

"Because they last for damn ever."

"You're cussing," Zoe chided gently.

"They're adventure games. Mommy wouldn't let him say bad words, either."

Zoe took a long, slow breath. "You sound kinda lonely, little fella. It's rough losing your mom. I know because I was just about your age when I lost mine."

Noah handed her his electronic game. "Do you know how to play?"

She shook her head. "But you could teach me."

"How'd your mother die?" Noah whispered.

Tony sucked in a deep breath. "Of all the low-down, dirty tricks to tell my kid about your—"

"In a wreck," she said simply.

Noah's blue eyes widened. He placed a hand on her knee.

"Only, I lost my daddy, too," she said.

Black boots shifted impatiently.

"How?" The word trembled on Noah's lips.

"Same car accident," she whispered. "They'd gone to a movie they said I was too little to see. When they died, I went to live with my mother's sister-in-law, Patty." Zoe spoke matter-of-factly, covering a wealth of pain. As a little girl she felt so lost and alone, so afraid that if she ever loved again, she'd suffer the same loss.

"Patty Creighton, who takes me for rides every time she gets a new red Cadillac?" Noah asked.

"Which is every damn year, thanks to you," Tony muttered savagely. "That money could go into the land."

''My land,'' Zoe reminded him.

''I lease it.''

Zoe ignored Tony and nodded at Noah. ''Only, back then Aunt Patty was an old maid and didn't know much about kids. But she had lots and lots of cats at her ranch. Seventeen. Maybe more. To keep the snakes away, she said. And she was a librarian, who didn't make much money or ever have a new car. But she took me with her to the library. That's when I began to read. All the time. To forget about my parents....''

''But it's hard to forget, and I don't want to forget,'' Noah said.

She'd read books instead of making friends. Then Tony had come along.

''You know what my favorite thing in all the world is?'' Zoe asked.

''No,'' Noah whispered.

''To lie, curled up with a cat in my lap, reading a book.''

''You have a cat?''

''Super Cat,'' she explained. ''He's home with a cat-sitter.''

''Dad won't let me have a cat.'' When Noah slanted his eyes toward his father, Zoe gave Tony a long, hard look, too.

''Cats make him sneeze,'' Tony said.

'''Cause I'm allergic.'' Noah sucked in a breath. ''But I like to play video games. 'Specially adventure, warrior games.''

''And you'll teach me if we sit together,'' she said eagerly.

''Stop it. Both of you,'' Tony roared. ''This budding friendship ends now. She won't be playing games or sitting by anybody.'' He turned on Zoe with a vengeance. ''I don't give a damn what scheme you hatched with my mother.''

''You're cussing again. He's a child.''

''My bad habits are none of your business.''

''You're a father. You have to try—''

''I said—don't lecture me about—''

''I wouldn't have met him if you hadn't lost him.''

Tony moved so close to her she could smell the hot, masculine scent of his powerful body as well as his minty cologne. She would've retreated, but she wasn't about to show cowardice.

Fortunately, the flight attendants called her row number.

''You and I were done with each other nine years ago, and you know it!'' Tony muttered heatedly. ''Let's keep it that way!''

''Fine.''

She caught her breath as he grabbed a bewildered Noah up in his arms and stomped off to a far corner of the lounge.

Noah's game was on the floor forgotten. She started to call to them and then thought better of it. Instead she slipped the game into her carry-on and rushed to the gate.

In spite of seat assignments, there seemed to be great confusion in boarding. Nevertheless, Zoe found her seat, which was a middle seat between a fat lady, who sat by the window and reeked of garlic, and an empty aisle seat. Hopefully, the flight wouldn't be full, and she could move into the aisle seat.

Lowering her head, Zoe pulled out her paperback and began to read. Thus, she was minding her own business, thank you very much, Mr. Big, Bad Cowboy, when suddenly Noah sprang into the empty seat beside her and buckled his seat belt.

"Hi," he said, flashing his toothy grin at her.

"Hi, yourself." She hesitated. "Where's your daddy?"

"Right here," drawled that deep, husky voice that made the bottom drop out of her stomach. "You're in my seat."

"My seat!" she snapped back at him.

His long, tanned fingers flapped a boarding pass in her face.

"Oh, dear, it does seem to have my seat number printed in bold black." She sighed.

"So, get up."

"There has to be a mistake."

Passengers stacked up behind him while she rummaged in her messy purse to find her mutilated boarding pass. When she got it out and unfolded it, she gasped.

"It's the same as mine!" he said.

"I got here first," she muttered. "So, the seat's mine."

"I need to sit by my son. Don't make me bodily remove you." He leaned across Noah. Her smile died when blunt fingertips unhooked her seat belt.

"Don't you dare touch her, Dad."

"He's right." She was shivering again from his nearness and from the accidental brushing of his hand against hers. "Be a gentleman and go ask the flight attendant for help."

"She speaks Greek."

"Your problem. I got here first."

Everybody glared at him. Even Noah.

"All right." Tony vanished toward the back of the plane.

All too soon he was back with a pretty flight attendant, who seemed to have a weakness for lethal, male beauty of the rugged, cowboy variety.

"Ma'am, I'm afraid you'll have to move," she said. "We've found a seat for you in the back of the plane."

"Where it's bumpy. Let the gentleman sit back there."

"But this little boy is his son."

"He's...my, er, my great-nephew," Zoe fought back tartly.

"And I want to sit with my aunt," Noah said, inspired. "We don't see each other very often, and we're going to play games."

"Sir, I don't understand. Duke? Her name *is* the same as yours."

"Noah!" Anthony barked. "She's no aunt! You never saw her before in your life."

"She's my aunt Zoe, and you know it!"

"Noah!"

"You said so yourself! And how come she's got my game, then, Dad?"

"The hell she does."

"Don't cuss at my great-nephew—nephew!"

Two more flight attendants appeared only to add to the confusion with dramatic hand gestures and rapid Greek. Both women batted their lashes at Tony, which made Zoe go green.

When Zoe still refused to move, the flirtatious blond flight attendant rushed to the front of the plane. Almost immediately the captain's deep voice boomed over the speaker system in English.

"We can't take off until all passengers are seated."

Zoe pulled Noah's game out of her bag, waved it at the boy. "You were going to teach me how to play."

"Oh, boy!" Noah said brightly as he deftly punched the on button. "First, you gotta know that there are all these warriors you can unlock. You want me to describe them?"

"Great!"

"Sit down, mister," said another passenger.

Tony gave Zoe another long appraisal, his eyes burning through layers of thick sweater with such scathing intensity that her nipples tingled.

"Be a gentleman," Zoe whispered.

"Okay. You win," Tony said. "For now."

Had she? Then why did her nipples feel as if they'd been burned with ice cubes all the way to Rhodes?

"Why can't Aunt Zoe go in our taxi?"

"She is not your aunt!"

"Yes, she is," Noah shrieked, circling round and round his father. "Remember, Nana told me about her at Madame Woo's."

"She can't go with us, Noah."

"I like her, Dad."

"That's because you don't know her as well as I do."

"She played with me the whole way over. She doesn't yawn and shift around in her seat like you do. She found me a pillow and a blanket when I got sleepy."

"She made me sit in the back of the plane."

"So?"

No way was Tony about to admit flying made him nervous, especially when the flying got bumpy.

"Because of her I was squeezed into a seat that wouldn't recline. The cushion was as hard as a rock and the size of a postage stamp. I had a fat man on either side of me...."

Noah yawned, so Tony didn't tell him that the fat men's beefy arms had overflowed into his space. Or that one of them had bad breath and had crunched potato chips the whole way. Or that when the flight had gotten bumpy, Tony had clenched the armrest so tightly, the men had laughed at him.

Glass doors of the terminal swung open, and a slim woman with auburn hair walked out into the bright sunshine with her backpack. That skintight, short, black mini clung to her shapely hips. Full breasts jiggled beneath her black sweater.

She'd walked like that in high school.

Do you have to make 'em bounce, baby?

"Shh." Tony knelt over the kid. "Here she comes. Look the other way. Don't you dare say anything about sharing a taxi."

She beamed when she saw Noah.

"Nephews!"

Tony thought of his uncle Duncan, and the word galled.

Noah waved wildly.

She took that as an invitation and stepped toward Tony, into his space. God, she smelled sweet. Lilacs. Way better than the fat men. And, oh, how her auburn hair flashed in the sun.

"Is this fate?" She ruffled Noah's hair, and the brat smiled from ear to ear, showing off his brand-new permanent teeth that were going to cost a fortune to straighten.

"Or is this fate?" she purred softly against Tony's ear. When he tensed, she whirled away, breasts bouncing. Then she smiled so flirtatiously at their dark driver the old fool's tongue nearly lolled out of his mouth.

"What do you bet we're all going to the same hotel?" She flapped her hotel voucher at the driver with a bright smile.

Noah pulled out an identical voucher.

"What'd I tell you?" she said.

The taxi driver grinned from ear to ear. "You could share—"

"You win the second round," Tony conceded. Bowing low, he opened the door for her.

"Romantic holiday?" the driver queried. "Second honeymoon?"

"We're not sure what it is yet," Zoe answered brightly as if the flight with Noah and their new friendship had made her overconfident.

But, oh, her hair was the color of spun flame beneath the bright Greek sun. And those breasts! And she smelled so good.

"Just get in the back seat," Tony growled as he took her luggage.

"My pleasure."

Then she winked at him.

"Don't flirt!"

"Maybe I can't help myself."

Four

"Nice," Zoe murmured.

Deliberately avoiding the dark eyes of the tall, dark man sitting on the patio next to hers, she slid her glass door open. She felt dangerously inspired to do mischief as she pranced past Tony in a skimpy black bikini and a loose, overlarge, white shirt that was sheer and soft after years of washings. She leaned against her low wall and eyed the blue-green Aegean and the mountains of Turkey and then stretched with feline grace, breathing in the cool, salty, humid air.

The shirt whipped around her, revealing her belly and slim waist.

"Too nice." Bitter sarcasm coated Tony's compliment.

Even though she didn't look his way, Zoe had the disquieting sensation he was watching her as she leaned back against her wall. She shaded her face with her hand so he couldn't see her blush.

"You're enjoying this," Tony accused crossly.

They had checked in together. Since they shared the same last name, the entire staff had assumed they were married and had just wanted lots of room. Then Zoe had explained everything in vivid detail that had made Tony turn the most darling shade of purple.

"So, you see, guys, I'm actually Tony's beloved aunt Zoe."

She'd rung a little bell and insisted Tony share her bellman, saying it was the least she could do since he'd been such a gentleman about the taxi. Then she'd given Noah her key and invited him inside to explore her unit, which he said he preferred to his father's.

"Am I staying with you, Aunt Zoe?"

"No," his father growled.

"You can come over anytime," she'd told Noah as Tony was dragging him away by the collar to their unit.

"The hell he can."

"You're cussing—"

"If you don't stop, you'll drive me to do worse...."

"I am breathless with anticipation. But why don't we both change into something more comfortable first?"

"What is that supposed to mean?"

"Whatever you want it to."

When she'd smiled, he'd stared at her, stunned. She'd shut her door in his face, her heart pounding. What in the world had gotten into her?

Their condominiums were located on the bottom

floor of a boxy, multistoried building that was painted a dazzling white. Both units looked out on a grassy lawn, an aqua swimming pool, a jewel-white strip of beach littered with blue and white umbrellas and chaise longues on the shores of the Aegean.

You're enjoying this, he'd said right before she'd gotten lost in her own thoughts.

Zoe inhaled a long breath. "What's not to enjoy? I don't have a problem with purple mountains of Turkey misting across the Aegean. Did you know they are exactly eleven miles away?"

If he'd been reading his guidebook as diligently as she had, he didn't say so.

"Or a problem with red bougainvillea dripping from all the balconies," she went on. "Or yellow roses and sprigs of basil frothing at my window boxes."

"Frothing." His chair legs grated against tile. "You've been editing too many novels."

"What if I have?" She plopped herself down in a chaise longue. "I am on vacation. One is supposed to enjoy one's vacation. Did you know Ulysses once sailed this very same sea on his way home from Troy?"

Tony leaned over the low white wall that separated their patios. He wore cutoffs and nothing else. He was dark all over, and his teak-brown belly was still as flat as a washboard. A strip of black hair ran up his middle and flared across his broad chest. He didn't used to have that much hair.

He looked too good, so doggone good and primitively male that her nerves skittered as if she'd taken a heady jolt of electricity. In nine years she hadn't felt this alive.

"Why, he looks good enough to eat."

"You're doing it. You're doing it."

His black eyes made a tour of her long, shapely legs. "What?" he muttered.

"I didn't say anything," she replied on a quick blush.

"Yes, you did. You were muttering to yourself. I used to think that was cute."

"Your imagination, cowboy."

His handsome mouth quirked. Oh, dear, there was that beguiling lopsided smile she used to think belonged only to her.

"You still talk to yourself, don't you?" he whispered in that raspy voice that had once belonged only to her, as well.

"Do not."

"Still make up stories?" he taunted. "Still want to write?"

She had brought a yellow legal pad and several pens. She had planned to try her hand while she was here. Not that her unrealized dreams were his concern.

"Is it true what they say about editors being frustrated writers?" he persisted.

"My life is none of your business."

"How about other frustrations?" His eyes burned over her body again.

Her color heightened. "I said mind your own—"

One black brow arched. "And if you'd minded yours, we wouldn't be here together. Did you or did you not set me up?" he demanded.

"Did you or did you not set me up?" she mimicked, winking at him flirtatiously. "You know *I* didn't!"

"Mammalian trickery."

"What is that supposed to mean?"

"That anything's possible especially where women are concerned. Especially a woman who married an old man who was her aunt's suitor."

"An old man who'd just discovered he was dying and wanted to exit Shady Lomas with a real bang."

"...A woman who became a millionairess when her husband obliged her by dying so fast."

"I told you—he did what he did on purpose. He used me to get back at you and his daughters. If his own family had accepted him—"

"So your marriage is my fault?"

She wet her lips nervously. "Look. I could have gone home to Shady Lomas if I'd wanted to be slapped in the face with my life history every time I turned around. We're here. And it wasn't easy to leave the office or my cat or be hand-searched in half a dozen airports. I for one intend to make the best of it—even if you're here, too."

"Even if I'm here. You got my mother to get me here...."

"You are too conceited to believe. True—you're kinda cute."

"Kinda?" He actually looked hurt.

"But, kinda cute or not, you are—understand this once and for all—you are the very last person I would choose to take a vacation with. I did not conspire with my aunt and your mother. They must have cooked this wacky plan up all by themselves because we're both single. We can either make the best of it or the worst of it. It's a long way home, so I suggest that you sit down and be quiet and pretend you know how to be a gentleman and let me enjoy these purple mountains across our wine-dark sea.''

''Wine-dark?'' He snorted.

''Homer. Hello? Do you read? *The Iliad.*''

''And *The Odyssey.* That water is blue, Miss Know-it-all Bookworm.''

''I wish you'd quit looking at my legs.''

''I would—if you'd stop blushing every time I do.''

''Quit looking, and I'll stop.''

Obediently he stared out to sea, too. She tried to imagine ancient Persian war galleys, their oars driven by shackled slaves, racing across the waves.

''You really didn't set me up?'' he persisted.

''End of that discussion. I am trying to relax and enjoy my vacation.''

''The only way to do that is to avoid each other.''

''So punish me,'' she said. ''Avoid me. Go inside.''

''Why don't you? We could take turns.''

''Turns? We sound like children. We've got adjoining condos, adjoining time-shares, whatever—thanks to your mother and my conniving aunt. You and I have known each other since the beginning of time. We could try just to make the best of a bad situation. After all, you are my nephew.''

''Just stop with the nephew bit.''

''Okay.'' She held up her hands in a defensive gesture. ''Okay. Truce. Your precious Noah, nimble-fingered Noah, is my new best friend. All I'm saying is that just because our high school romance went sour—''

''You slept with me and married my rich uncle, who I don't claim, by the way.''

"Because you slept with me and the next time I saw you, Rene was all tangled up in your arms and legs."

"Any girl with two eyes could've seen that I was trying to get loose. You accused me to get yourself off the hook."

"No. Because of Rene and you, I did what I did. I know I was stupid, but that's why I did it."

"You're not off the hook."

"Okay, but do we have to hate each other for the whole week? Maybe the only week we'll ever be here?"

He stared at her and then at the Aegean. Maybe the sheer, spectacular beauty of this idyllic paradise was beginning to get to him as it was to her.

"I came here to figure out my future," she said. "If you don't hush and leave me alone, I'll never be able to think about anything." She smiled at him. "How about some ouzo?"

"I will not drink ouzo with you."

"Your loss." She poured herself a glass, shifted her chaise longue so she couldn't see him, stared at the mountains and began to sip.

Even before he spoke, she was burningly conscious of his gaze on her legs again. He laughed when she blushed.

"You can just feel me looking at you, can't you?"

Her cheeks got hotter. "Would you quit?"

"It's called chemistry."

"I don't care what it is called. Just quit."

"Where'd you get that?" he demanded. "The ouzo, I mean."

"I ordered it off a menu last night. It was so good I bought a bottle. I was jet-lagged as all get-out. After a sip or two, I felt absolutely mellow. It tastes weird, like licorice, but it's great."

Noah skipped out onto the balcony and ran up to the wall beside Zoe. Blue eyes peered over into her patio. "Can I have a drink, too?"

"No," Tony replied.

She got up. The wind sent her shirt sailing above her head. When it fell back into place, the blaze in Tony's eyes made her feel so positively naked, she shuddered and then rewarded him with an all-body flush.

"O-of course you can, Noah, dear. I have juice and soft drinks in my fridge." She smiled at both her male fans before heading inside.

"He can get his own damn drink out of our fridge."

"He's cussing at me again," Noah tattled as he shoved a plastic chair over to the white wall that divided their balconies. He climbed onto the wall where he sat, skinny legs dangling over her side.

Zoe returned with a tall glass of frosty orange juice.

"I'd rather have a soda," Noah said, poking a straw into the bubbles.

"You'll drink what she brought and say thank-you," Tony growled.

"Thank you." Instead of drinking, Noah set the glass on the edge of the wall. She touched his knee that was red from his fall, and he smiled at her bashfully.

Noah was incredibly adorable. Oh, dear, dear. She had it bad.

"Your father's afraid of flying. Did you know that?"

Noah shook his head and made his bangs flop. "That's why he's so grumpy."

"But he doesn't fly in Texas."

"You mean he's grumpy like this all the time?"

Noah looked at the ground sheepishly. "Well, most of the time, I guess."

Tony slammed a chair against the wall so hard, Noah's glass fell and shattered on Zoe's red-tiled patio. "It's hard to be happy, damn it, when—" Tony stopped, appalled by his outburst and the mess he made.

Zoe rushed toward him, her gaze on his ravaged face.

"When the wife you loved more than anything is dead," Zoe finished softly. "The only woman you ever…"

"Don't put words into my mouth. You don't know a damn thing about me anymore. Enjoy your precious balcony to yourself. Oh…sorry about the glass."

I know you go to the cemetery every week.

"Come on, Noah. We're going inside—"

When she'd cleaned up the breakage and was alone, she felt adrift and far lonelier than she had after she'd thrown Abdul out of her apartment a month ago.

Why had she pushed Anthony? But flirting with Anthony made her feel alive. His pain devastated her. How was that possible…unless…

She had seven days here. Maybe it was good in a way that this man who had haunted her for nine years was next door. Maybe if she faced him, she'd see him for the macho, pigheaded redneck he probably was. Then she'd get over him and be happy when she found some sophisticated, gentlemanly man more to her taste in Manhattan. One way or another she needed to grow up and move on.

She finished her ouzo and decided to go for a walk on the beach. The sand was fine and white and littered with perfect, round, white rocks. Clear, turquoise water lapped against the shoreline. Blue and white umbrellas had been lowered and were folded against their poles. Cushions had been stashed in a cabana, and the chaise longues were stacked under the building's eaves. A sea breeze whispered through her hair. She hadn't walked far before Noah dashed up to her.

"Does your father know where you are?"

He shook his bright head. "I think he's mad. He's just sitting in the kitchen not saying anything."

"You really shouldn't run off from him like this, you know."

He knelt in the sand and began inspecting the rocks that littered the beach.

"Look at all the perfect, round rocks." He built a mountain out of them while she stood over him and watched.

Soon, it was getting dark, and he'd stuffed his pockets until they were bulging with rocks. It would have been fun to romp with him in the sand, to take him to dinner, to play another adventure game with him. But he didn't belong to her. She wasn't his mother.

"I really think we should go find your father," she said.

"He likes being alone."

"We don't want him to worry, though."

"I don't care." Noah crossed his arms.

"You know you don't mean that."

She took him by the hand, and he wove his fingers through hers and clung tightly, as she led him home. They were halfway across the lawn to their condos when Anthony rushed up to them.

"I've been looking everywhere—"

"He followed me to the beach. I was just—"

"You should've known I'd be worried—"

"I did. I was just—"

"Dad, she was bringing me—"

"Home," she said gently.

"Then, thanks. Thanks a lot for being so nice to him." His eyes clung to her face for a long moment. Then he seized the boy, turned his back and abruptly left her.

She stood in the dark and watched them until they disappeared into the golden glow of their doorway. The door shut behind them. She leaned back against a tall palm with rustling fronds, staying there until the stars came out and the beach was quite dark. The lights went out at Tony's condo. They'd probably gone out to dinner.

Never, ever had she felt more alone.

Wrong.

The worst night of her life had been Tony's wedding night. She'd been a widow. And he'd married Rene, anyway.

Would she ever get over him?

Yes! She clenched her hands together. Her fingernails dug into her palms. She was going to dinner all by herself. She'd take her book. She'd eat grilled octopus and have a Greek salad. She was going to do what she'd come here to do—think.

If it was the last thing she ever did, she would

figure out how to rid herself of her hangup about Anthony Duke.

Old boyfriends. Who needed them? She, for one, was not going to be haunted by hers for the rest of her life.

Zoe had ruined his evening. It was late. All through that feast of souvlaki, Greek for shish kebabs, and grilled fish, which Anthony had washed down with too much retsina, wine flavored with pine resin, he'd moodily thought about her.

Zoe's condo was dark, but her patio doors were open. Her long white curtains swirled in the wind. It was just like her to go to bed and forget to close her doors.

What she did was none of his business. Still, Tony had knocked at her front door four times and grown even more worried and frustrated when he'd gotten no answer. If she were home, you'd think she'd answer.

He'd even called her. She hadn't answered her damn phone, either. Again, he reminded himself, she wasn't his concern. Still, he couldn't go to sleep with those patio doors open.

Anybody could see those curtains and go in and do anything to her. Maybe she'd picked somebody up. A stranger, a madman capable of anything.

A madman? Anthony knew he was losing it. But what if she'd fallen and couldn't get to the phone? He imagined her injured, semiconscious sprawled out on that gleaming, white-tiled floor.

On that happy thought, he jumped their wall, threw back her billowing curtains and stomped across her slick floor to check on her for himself.

He called her name in the darkened condo. Again, she didn't answer. When he punched at a light switch to get his bearings, the lights didn't come on.

Their condos were mirror opposites, so he knew the layout. Swiftly he made his way across her tiny living room, dining room, and kitchen. As he turned to the left and stepped into the hall, he heard her shower go off. A faint crack of light glimmered beneath her bathroom door.

Before he could retreat, the door opened, and he was enveloped in a warm, golden mist.

Run! She's fine.

His bare feet rooted themselves to the cold white tiles. The mist cleared. Like Venus in her seashell, Zoe was naked and more beautiful than ever. In one hand an apricot towel dangled to the floor.

He gulped in the scent of lilacs. Then he whispered her name. Before she could scream, he had her against the pink tile wall, his hand over her slick, hot lips.

"Shh. It's just me, Tony," he murmured gently. "I wouldn't hurt you. Not for the world. I was just making sure you're okay."

Her damp breasts mashed into his chest and soaked his shirt. Without really knowing what he was doing, his long fingers wound into her thick wet hair. Her heart beat wildly, but no more wildly than the drumbeats in his own chest. Instead of fighting him, she went still.

He knew he should let her go and apologize for scaring her, but he felt the mad need to touch her and hold her and make love to her. Suddenly she was melting into his heat even as he melted into hers.

"Tell me this is a dream. Tell me we're not really

doing this,'' she whispered even as she dropped her apricot-colored towel and arched herself into his body.

His whole world became hot, wet, flame-haired woman with the pixie face.

''It's a dream,'' he muttered roughly. ''The same nightmare that's tormented me for nine damn years.''

''You, too?''

''Yeah. Even down to the shower.''

''Apricot towel, too?'' she purred.

''I'll have to add that detail.''

''So will I. And I didn't realize the mist was from the shower.''

Her luminous brown eyes widened, whether with fear or desire, he didn't know. He was too far gone to care. He simply lowered his mouth to hers.

He knew he should stop, but his quickening breath told him it was already too late. Even before his lips touched hers and he caught that first delicious taste, he had to have more. Still, he waited a heartbeat.

''Stop me, why don't you?'' he muttered. ''Fight. Writhe!''

''Would you stop?'' She moaned and went limp. ''Can you stop? Can you?''

Her lush, warm body felt glued to his.

''Oh, Zoe...'' His voice was thick with need.

She opened her mouth and wet her lips and then his too with the tip of her tongue.

That second little taste of her even before he kissed her pushed him over some edge, and he was lost.

Then she said, ''Let's get you naked.''

He felt violently aroused, totally at her mercy.

''This is torture,'' he muttered.

"But sweet, mad torture," she promised, teasing him with a saucy grin. "So...enjoy."

He answered with a soft chuckle.

Their tongues touched. Then they kissed.

Five

One warm, wet kiss.

Make that one helluva kiss, Anthony silently amended as he stared at Zoe, who was flushed and naked and alluring and begging him to get naked, too.

This is wrong!

Maybe so, but as her big, brown eyes flicked over him in awe, Anthony felt something hot and dangerous luring him on. How the hell could he stop now? What man made of flesh and pumping blood could have?

She drew her tongue across her lips and then lifted a fingertip and toyed with the top button of his shirt, undoing it.

She married your bastard uncle. She got the ranch, the house, everything. Her aunt drives red Cadillacs just like Uncle Duncan used to, and that irritates the hell out of you. You lease her land—land that should be yours.

His body was sending him a different message as her hand moved beneath his shirt. Then she leaned forward and kissed him again.

Her lips clung to his, and he tasted her and reveled in doing so. Licorice? Ouzo? Whatever it was, his blood buzzed with desire.

"What are you doing here?" she whispered drowsily a few dozen kisses later as she levered herself forward into the hard, masculine strength of his body.

"You left your back doors wide open."

"And you took that as an invitation to…?" There was no mistaking the husky timbre in her voice as she slid her palms down his shoulders.

"Anybody could have."

"But anybody didn't. You did." Her hands moved over his muscles lovingly.

"I was worried."

"About little ol' me? You could've knocked."

"I did," he replied with quiet gravity. "I phoned, too. You didn't answer."

"Well, I'm okay, cowboy. You can go." Her teasing voice was deep and velvety.

Talk about mammalian trickery. She said one thing, but in the next breath she gave him that wide, lush smile.

"Is that really what you want?"

"What I want?" she purred. As if mesmerized by him, she threaded her fingers through his hair. "What I want—"

"Awhile ago you asked me to get naked."

"Are you sure you didn't maybe dream that up on your own?"

"Did you drink more of that ouzo stuff?"

She nodded and buried her face against his throat. "What I want? What I want is...so wrong." Her hot tongue flicked at the pulse beat in the hollow of his throat. "But now that you mention it, why don't you get naked."

His heart sped up. The tongue kept at it—flicking, twirling—until he couldn't breathe and his body was swollen and lava hot.

He gasped. "This is crazy."

She wiggled against his groin. Her voice was lower, sexier. "I don't know what I want," she said thickly.

"Well, maybe I do." His finger traced along her soft cheek, down her throat, down, down, circling over each nipple until they peaked into pert little beads of desire.

She shuddered. "You think so, huh? Let's see if you're still as hunky out of those clothes as you are in them."

Then she was peeling him out of his shirt, leaning into him, her slim fingers flying over those shirt buttons even faster than his, loosening, tearing. She was the one who tugged at the white sleeves, yanking his shirt off his brown shoulders. Then she ran her hands over sculpted muscle.

"So, the years have been kind. Oh, Anthony, why do you have to be built like a hunky god?"

"Talk about ego gratification," he muttered.

"Psychobabble from the big, bad cowboy." Giggling, she ran her hands down his naked spine. "I want to hate you. Did you know that's been my ambition for nine years?''

''Mine, too.'' He pulled her closer. ''We're not doing too good.''

''So, you thought about me?'' she asked.

''Not happy thoughts.''

''Then you think we're going to regret this in the morning?'' She rubbed her breasts back and forth against the black bristly hairs on his chest.

''Definitely.''

''But this sure feels good tonight.''

''Definitely.'' The soft feel of her naked flesh rocked him to the core. With a thudding heart, he whispered her name and put a question mark at the end of it. ''Zoe? Zoe?''

''Who's afraid of the big, bad cowboy?'' she hummed, letting him go. She leaned back against the wall and drew a deep, shuddering breath. ''Not me,'' she whispered in a tiny voice. ''Not me.''

The silence between them thickened.

''Are you afraid?'' he whispered.

She didn't answer for a long time. Did he only imagine that she shivered? ''You know me. I leap off the cliff and then look for a safe place to land.''

''While you're in the leaping mood, wrap your legs around my waist and hang on,'' he murmured dryly against her ear.

''Oh, dear.''

''Just do it.''

She leaped, and he caught her.

Her legs around his waist felt too good. She was sleek and slender, but he said, ''You've put on a pound or two.''

''So have you, buster.''

"In all the right places," he murmured.

She ran her hands over his muscular shoulders again. "Ditto."

Gripping her tightly at the waist, he carried her into the bedroom.

"This better be good," she challenged as he lowered her to the bed.

The mattress dipped beneath their weight. "Or what?"

"I have this thing for your hunky body."

"Just my body?"

"It'd be terrible to have a thing…and…and…"

"Shut up," he whispered gently as he ripped the sheets back. "Just shut up." He threw the pillows onto the floor.

"This isn't fair. We should be messing up your bedroom…."

His mouth crushed down on hers. And it wasn't long before she quit trying to make conversation about idiotic things like housekeeping details. He kissed her everywhere just like in his dream. And just like in his dreams, she kissed him back.

She wasn't as experienced in reality as the vixen he dreamed about, but her shy, awkward fumbling turned him on even more. Maybe she didn't do this with every guy on the block.

A surge of jealousy shook him at the mere thought of other men. Nine years. How many had there been? What about Uncle Duncan? He'd been a sick man when he'd married her. Had he even been able to consummate their marriage?

Don't think about it. Not now. Not when you've got her right where you want her, under you, writhing and twisting.

She moaned and arched her body against him. "Now. Now."

He laughed and slowed their pace and made her wait. When he wouldn't speed up, she kissed the middle of his chest. Then she bit him.

"Ouch."

"Now," she urged. "Now."

"You little wildcat..."

"Now. Get inside me. I can't wait."

He peeled a condom out of its wrapper and put it on. Straddling her, he thrust deeply.

She went still.

So did he.

"You okay?" he whispered.

She smiled, her face radiant.

Oh, the joy...the pleasure of those breathless, silent moments. He felt himself swell and heat up inside her. She gasped with pleasure. Then he began to rock back and forth and let the ecstasy build. She was soft and hot but gentle and loving too, and her hands were all over him.

Awkward with each other no longer, their bodies moved in that ageless, perfect rhythm. She felt so good. So damned good. So damned incredible. So perfect.

Nine years he'd gone without this. Nine years. He wanted their lovemaking to last forever. And it seemed that it might for a while. Then the pressure inside him built, but he held back, waiting for her even as passion swept through him. Waiting, his fists wound so tight they hurt, waiting until he was mad with desire and still she couldn't seem to—

He opened his eyes. Her lips moved. She was staring past him up at the Venetian chandelier. ''Ten, eleven, twelve little lightbulbs…''

Lightbulbs? Was she counting bulbs to herself under her breath?

''Stop it,'' he muttered savagely.

She gasped. Then he kissed her hard. When her body went wild, he spun crazily out of control, too. A second or two later, she exploded. He came after she did.

He wound his hands through her hair. ''Did I ever tell you I loved your hair?''

She was still trembling all over. ''Oh, Anthony…what have we done?''

''Counting? Those damn little lightbulbs? Why did you do that?''

''To make it last.''

''I thought I wasn't doing it right.'' His voice was oddly rough. He felt so damned vulnerable, and he hated that. She would use it…maybe to destroy him again.

She kissed the tip of his nose. ''How could you think that? You were too perfect to believe.''

She laid her head next to his shoulder and fell asleep.

''Too perfect.…''

With her warm body cuddled against him, and his desire sated, his brain went into overdrive. He remembered every sordid detail of the past, especially the details involving her marriage to that scoundrel, Uncle Duncan, and her inheritance, the Duke inheritance.

His inheritance.

She and her aunt had made him the laughingstock of Shady Lomas. He'd plunged into marriage with

Rene, the prettiest girl in town, just to prove he hadn't cared. But he had cared, and he'd made Rene so unhappy. She'd loved him, and he'd hurt her so badly he'd have Rene's unhappiness on his conscience forever.

Zoe slept as blissfully as a baby in his arms while he lay beside her, staring up at the ceiling for hours. It wasn't so easy to forget those red Cadillacs Zoe's aunt Patty bought every year while his own mother had to drive an old truck that had over two-hundred-thousand miles on it. Or to forget that he leased Zoe's land, prime Duke ranchland, from her aunt to run his cattle on.

When he finally fell asleep, he dreamed he was in a red Cadillac convertible. He and Zoe were parked in a pasture choked with mesquite and aflame with bluebonnets. They were making love in the back seat.

When he woke up, it was dawn. Zoe's cheek was pressed against his hair, and he was breathing hard.

A damned red Cadillac! They'd done it in Duncan's damn red Cadillac!

Careful not to disturb her, Anthony got up, grabbed his clothes, pulled on his slacks, locked all of Zoe's doors and stalked back to his own condo.

"A damned red Cadillac!" he muttered as he stripped and got in his shower.

No way in hell was he going to get involved with Zoe Creighton. Make that Zoe Duke! Make that Aunt Zoe! After all, she'd married Uncle Duncan!

Zoe's bedroom glowed gold with a magical light. For a hazy moment she had no idea where she was. All she knew was that she felt warm and cozy and

Silhouette Reader Service™ — Here's how it works:

g your 2 free books and mystery gift places you under no obligation to buy anything. You may keep the books and return the shipping statement marked "cancel." If you do not cancel, about a month later we'll send you 6 al books and bill you just $3.57 each in the U.S., or $4.24 each in Canada, plus 25¢ shipping & handling per book icable taxes if any.* That's the complete price and — compared to cover prices of $4.25 each in the U.S. and ch in Canada — it's quite a bargain! You may cancel at any time, but if you choose to continue, every month we'll u 6 more books, which you may either purchase at the discount price or return to us and cancel your subscription.

and prices subject to change without notice. Sales tax applicable in N.Y. Canadian residents will be charged e provincial taxes and GST.

BUSINESS REPLY MAIL

FIRST-CLASS MAIL PERMIT NO. 717-003 BUFFALO, NY

POSTAGE WILL BE PAID BY ADDRESSEE

SILHOUETTE READER SERVICE
3010 WALDEN AVE
PO BOX 1867
BUFFALO NY 14240-9952

incredibly wonderful. Maybe Aunt P and Ursula had been right to advise Greece.

Then she sat up and realized she was naked and her bed was a mess. Her vision was a little blurry. Was that her apricot towel all tangled up in the doorway? Whatever was it doing there?

An image sprang full-blown into her mind. She was naked, and Anthony was pushing her hot body back against that icy wall.

"This is bad.... It's a dream." Her voice grew softer and more desperate. "Please let it be a dream...." For no reason at all she couldn't stop looking at that towel.

She saw her hand opening, and felt the towel slipping out of it, right before he'd grabbed her.

Why did her body feel so...so different... somehow...so complete?

Oh, dear. She'd drunk several glasses of ouzo at dinner.

More visions rose to torment her. In her dream...was it a dream...well, whatever...she'd crawled on top of Tony and kissed her way down, all the way down from his broad, brown forehead to...to his shaft.

She remembered a mat of thick, black whorls at his groin. He'd been so huge. Huge! She put her hand to her lips. What was that funny taste in her mouth?

"Oh, dear! You didn't!"

"You did!"

"You're doing it!"

"Shut up!"

She wrenched the sheets up to her neck. Even so, she couldn't stop shaking. After a dream like that, how would she face him today? And Noah?

"It was only a dream!"

But when she got up and went to the bathroom and picked up her damp, apricot towel, certain delicate tissues of her body felt raw and used as they rubbed together. She clutched the towel to her breasts. Then her legs went limp at the knees when she saw her face in the mirror.

"Oh, God…oh, God…"

Her hair was a mess. When she pressed a fingertip to her swollen lips, her temples began to pound.

No dream! She'd done it with him!

Warm sexual afterglow mixed with wild panic.

"What are you going to do about this, big girl?"

"Get your skinny fanny on a fast jet back to Manhattan!" said a wise sassy voice.

"You're doing it."

"Shut up! Shut up—both of you! I've got to think!"

She grabbed her white, terry-cloth robe off a hook, put it on and stumbled into her kitchen where she made coffee and boiled herself an egg. Then she opened a container of yogurt and poured honey and walnuts into the rich stuff.

She sat down to eat, but just as she dipped her spoon into the thick, velvety yogurt oozing with honey and walnuts, her phone rang.

Her hand froze, her spoon sinking slowly into the golden goo.

No way could she face Anthony so soon!

Maybe it wasn't him. Of course it was him.

On the fifth ring she placed her hand on the receiver, but she just sat there, her pulse racing, as she stared unseeingly out the window at the aqua pool and sea and those incredible lavender mountains. The sun was already brilliant in a cloudless blue sky. Again, the water was that same shade of dazzling blue green. Indeed, the whole world seemed to sparkle.

Scarcely had the phone stopped jingling and she'd lifted her spoon again than her doorbell rang. She dropped her spoon with a plunk, splattering little globs of yogurt all over the table.

Would the big lug ever give up?

She stomped to the door, clutched her robe around her neck and shouted through the thick wood, "You got what you wanted last night! Now go away!"

"It's just me," said a soft, crushed voice.

She unlocked the door. "*Noah.* Oh, dear! Darling, I'm sorry."

She meant to crack the door a mere inch, but the minute she turned the knob, Anthony shoved the toe of his black boot in it.

She slammed the door.

"Ouch!"

"You're hurting him, Aunt Zoe."

Zoe decided there was nothing to do but open it wider. She stepped back as Anthony stormed inside.

"Talk about mammalian trickery!" she whispered in a goaded undertone.

Blue eyes bright, Noah smiled up at her. "We want you to spend the day with us, Aunt Zoe."

"Doing what?" she replied, her voice raw as she held the edges of her robe together.

"Anything you want," Anthony murmured so sexily she itched to slap him.

"You should be ashamed," she pleaded.

"Me? About last night? You have no room to talk!"

"I meant to use your son to get through my door."

"Oh, this was his idea."

"I'll bet."

"It was," Noah confirmed. "Just like it was my idea to sit by you on the plane and to get you to share our taxi!"

"See!" said his father, grinning down at her.

Oh, dear. As always Tony's lopsided smile got through all her defenses.

"You're incorrigible," she whispered, her voice cracking.

"Ditto."

She glared up at Anthony.

Again, his triumphant smile was so charmingly crooked, it took her breath away.

Noah stared at them both. As if sensing he was out of his depth, he squinted and then looked away, wary all of sudden.

Oh, dear. Anthony's black eyes shone even brighter than they had last night. They were so hot and dark, she felt consumed in the same crazy flame that had devoured her.

"I...I..."

"We knew you'd say yes, so I've rented a little car and ordered three picnic lunches from the resort cafeteria."

She'd been trying to forget Anthony Duke for nine long years. "I couldn't possibly," she said forcing an edge in her voice.

"What will it take to change your mind?" Anthony demanded softly.

"Nothing. You couldn't possibly—"

"Noah, why don't you go play your adventure

game in our condo while I talk to your Aunt Zoe…in private.''

''Sure, Dad—''

''Noah!'' she cried desperately. ''Don't you dare leave me alone with him.''

''Noah!'' His father's tone was stern. ''Remember our deal?''

Father and son exchanged a look. If Noah had been a magic genie capable of vanishing in a puff of smoke, he couldn't have disappeared faster. The door soon slammed behind Noah, and she was alone with Anthony.

Six

"We hate each other," Zoe said, her pulse accelerating now that she was alone with Anthony in her kitchen.

"Did you sleep well?" he asked, his deep tone laced with polite concern. "I had some disturbing dreams."

"Just leave. You know we don't even like each other."

"I told myself that too when I got up this morning."

"See, you dislike me, too."

Still, just a few hours ago, they'd made love in the adjoining bedroom. Oh, dear. Why hadn't she made the bed?

"My heart's thundering like a jackhammer. Is that what I feel—dislike?" he whispered.

When his possessive gaze raked her naked shoulder, she clutched the edges of her robe together again.

''What are you wearing under that robe? Not much, I hope.''

Zoe swallowed. A dull red crept up her neck as she adjusted her robe again to cover herself.

''Mmm. Does anything in the whole world... maybe besides lilacs...smell as good as fresh coffee brewing? Do you mind if I pour myself a cup?''

''I just wish you'd go.''

Instead of leaving, he opened her cabinet and banged cups madly before pulling one out. She felt strange, all mixed up as he moved about, making himself at home in her kitchen, rummaging in a drawer for a spoon and then dipping it into the sugar bowl.

Was he staking a claim? Or had he done that last night? His every assured movement as he poured milk and stirred in sugar implied all the new intimacies that bound them and yet tormented her, too.

''No way can I go anywhere with you today,'' she said as primly as she could manage.

He sat down and added more sugar to his coffee, his spoon clanging so vigorously against the delicate cup, she was afraid it might shatter. Abruptly he dropped his spoon just as noisily in his saucer.

''What about last night, Zoe?'' His eyes went dark and intense as if he were searching into her heart.

She lowered her lashes so he couldn't read her secrets. ''What about it?'' she whispered in a trembling tone.

''What did it mean?'' he demanded.

''Mean?'' she repeated, picking up her cup and

twisting it round and round in her fingers. She felt shaky, so she pulled out a chair and sat down beside him.

"So you sleep around in Manhattan, do you?"

"Why, how dare you accuse—" She set her cup in her saucer and flashed him a hot look.

He laughed. "Then there must've been some reason that you…that I…"

She could feel the vein in her neck throbbing. "You came into my condo. I…I was naked."

"Delightfully so." He smiled as if he relished the despicable memory, but one glance into her huge, luminous eyes, and his smile died.

"You grabbed me," she accused. "You took advantage—"

"So…you're saying that what happened meant nothing to you, and that it was all my fault." His deep voice was dangerously quiet.

"That sounds good. Really good." She nodded her head briskly, hoping he'd buy it and go.

"You little liar. We made love for hours, and you know it. If anything, you were more enthusiastic than I—"

"I certainly was not!"

She shoved her cup and saucer across the table and got up. She meant to run from him and get dressed in her bedroom, but his hand snaked across the kitchen table and grabbed her wrist.

"You were wild about me, and I'll prove it!"

When he drew her closer, her robe fell off her shoulder again. She fought to readjust it, but his hand got there first.

"A gentleman would go," she said.

"I'm a cowboy, remember?" Sliding his rough

palm across her bare skin, his fingers heated as he pulled the robe lower. "You're naked under this, aren't you?"

"Why are you here this morning?" she pleaded. "Why won't you just leave me alone?"

"Would you have preferred me to have treated last night as a one-night stand and gone off somewhere with Noah and just ignored you?"

No! Yes! No!

Instead of answering him, she bit her bottom lip until it bled. He was impossible. Every single answer was impossible. The whole situation was…

She notched her chin upward and eyed him defiantly. "Are you just after more sex?"

"Are you suggesting more sex?" He smiled.

"Stop." She bit her tongue, and the taste of copper in her mouth grew stronger. "I…I shouldn't have asked you such a leading question."

"I didn't mind. If you're thinking about sex, I want to know." He burst out laughing. Then he pulled her closer. "You've still got the hots for me, and that makes you madder than hell."

Fingers splayed, she pushed against his chest, but he was strong and had no intention of releasing her.

"More sex sounds good." He grinned. "It's been a while. Rene and I…we weren't—"

"I'm sorry…about Rene." Zoe remembered how sick Rene had been. Last night hadn't been special to him. Zoe had just been a convenience after a long, forced abstinence.

"And you were really, really good," he murmured. "*We* were good."

"There is no 'we.'" Why couldn't she speak normally? Why was her voice so choked?

"You sure about that?"

"Just go. Please...just go."

"Then how will *we* ever know?" His dark gaze roamed her face, lingering on her naked shoulder.

"Know what?"

"What it all meant."

"I told you. It meant nothing."

He sighed. "I wish you were right. Maybe you do, too. I don't think it's that simple." His arms wound around her waist. Instead of fighting him, she stood perfectly still as she had last night and let him mold her against his muscular body as if she belonged there.

It all felt strangely right and thrilling to be in his arms. Her nerves sang. How she'd loved him when she'd been a girl.

Oh, dear. She had it bad.

"You hate me for marrying your uncle," she accused. "And I hate you...for choosing Rene. For being so deliriously happy with her...while I—"

Anthony cursed under his breath, but he didn't release her. "Yes, I hate that you married Duncan and made me the laughingstock of Shady Lomas. I was pretty self-righteous back then, and I guess folks needed a laugh. Maybe this whole thing was good for my character."

"You? The laughingstock? You were married to beautiful, perfect Rene."

"Why do you think I married her?"

"Because she was beautiful and perfect... and...and..."

"Too damned perfect," he muttered.

"It's me, the black widow, the shady lady of Shady Lomas, that everybody gossips about."

"Not just you, honey. They take me down a peg or two every chance they get. They said you went from me to him. You should hear Guy Pearsol's jokes on the subject when he ties one on."

"Guy's gross."

"But he's funny...when it's at someone else's expense."

"He really makes jokes about you?"

"Why'd the bookworm leave you, Duke? The only thing stiff about Duncan was his joints? Answer—new dollar bills are stiff. How do you feel about her being the owner of Duke Ranch and a glamorous New York editor to boot?"

"Oh, dear...." Zoe hesitated. "I'm sorry. I don't go home because I can't face— And you have to live there...."

"Sometimes I envy you because you got out. Rene was perfect, but I wasn't the perfect husband for her. Far from it. Then I've got Mother and my cousins to take care of. And there's Noah, too."

"So, will you go back and tell everybody that you've had the last laugh?"

"What do you mean?"

"Will you tell them we did it?"

"Is that what you think? That this is some kind of game to me?" His voice was deep and dark. So were his troubled eyes. "What we did... Well, it's nobody's damn business but ours what we did."

The way he said it, the way he looked at her made her feel so special.

Then his roughened hands were in her hair. "Zoe. I woke up this morning hating you...and wanting you. Mostly wanting you and hating myself because of it. Baby, you've damn sure got me in a tailspin."

"I know the feeling."

He lifted a strand of silk, and the Greek sun turned it to flame. "Then Noah said he wanted to spend the day with you and that I'm not as much fun as you are."

"That's brutal."

"Yeah. From the mouths of babes. But the truth is, I'd have more fun, too, if you came."

"You would?"

"If it was only about sex last night, I wouldn't feel that way, would I?"

"I never was very good at reading minds."

Before she could really get going on her argument, he drew her closer. Without even a thought to resistance, she lifted her lips to meet his.

His mouth closed over hers, sweetly, gently. Not hungrily like last night. Her lips parted with matching, heartfelt need. It felt so good to be held and kissed at breakfast the morning after.

"What is going on here?" whispered one of those little warning voices inside.

"Shut up. Shut up."

"You could write off last night. This morning is serious."

"Shut up."

"You're doing it."

Anthony's mouth on hers silenced the voices. Soon her whole body was trembling with sensual delight as his lips continued to kiss hers tenderly. She half opened her mouth, and his tongue slid inside. Her breathing was soon as uneven and harsh as his.

Her arms came around his shoulders. She couldn't resist winding his soft black hair at his nape around her fingertip. Nobody ever had made her feel even half as wonderful as he did.

She still loved him!

Love?

That word covered a lot of bases. Still, whatever she felt…

This was bad.

Oh, dear. Oh, dear…dear…dear…

"Let me go," she whispered pleadingly, knowing that if he picked her up and carried her to bed she, spineless ninny that she was—no, make that sex-starved nympho, at least where he was concerned—she wouldn't do anything to stop him.

"Let you go? Now that I have found you? I have a much better idea."

"I'm afraid to ask."

"Let's play show and tell."

"I don't know what you mean."

"Not to worry. I'll show you…."

Gently he lowered her back into her kitchen chair.

"What are you doing?"

"Not to worry," he muttered with a wry smile.

Then he was down on his knees and crawling under the table toward her lap before she could protest. When she tried to get up, his hands clamped around her waist, holding her in place.

"What—" She stiffened and brought her legs together.

"Relax," he whispered, putting his hands on her knees and opening her legs.

Before she could think of another ploy to stop him, his mouth blazed a trail from her knee up her thigh. Up…up… He was going all the way.

He spread her legs, his expert lips lingering in all

those intimate spots a nice girl would never let a man anywhere near. His tongue found forbidden lips and made nerves she'd never known she had flame and tingle and come to life full of new needs. He kept kissing her until the pleasure down there grew nearly unbearable.

She gasped, squirming in her wooden chair. Then her hands cupped his black head. Every flick of his tongue, every wet, darting kiss made her blood pulse faster. She was soon so hot, she felt steam must be seeping out of every pore.

This is bad. I can't blame this on ouzo.

Then his unerring mouth found her most sensitive spot and toyed with it, taking her to some rosy nirvana, a paradise beyond thought and doubt. The perfumed air of this insanely delicious heaven smelled of spring roses. She was near the summit, flying weightlessly, melting and moaning softly, when his tongue and callused hands stopped.

Abruptly, she fell to earth like a brick.

Faster than she could blink, he had scrambled into his chair and was stirring his coffee with a well-practiced air of gentlemanly innocence.

She took her cue, pulled her robe together and sat up ramrod straight in a more ladylike posture. Her heart was still knocking, and she couldn't look at him without blushing. Still, she stuck a spoon into her yogurt and lifted her cup and swallowed her cold, black coffee.

The front door slammed open and Noah came running in.

Anthony must have ears like a lynx.

"Dad, is she coming? Is she?"

Coming? Her skin flamed at the word.

''No,'' she said, not daring to look at Anthony for fear she'd really turn beet red. ''And, Tony, tell him that's definite. Please…tell him…and…and just go.''

''Noah, it's your turn to ask her. I did my best…to work my…er…charms on her.'' The incorrigible beast smiled at her in that lopsided way that made her heart flip. ''Now it's your turn, son.''

''You're dangerous,'' she muttered to Anthony. ''You know that, don't you?''

''I try.''

''You don't play fair.''

''Who's playing?'' he murmured silkily.

She could still feel his tongue rasping over her silky sex, still feel his roughened hands doing all those delicious things to her lower body that had her wet with desire.

As if he read her mind, Anthony smiled at her wickedly. Then he downed a long swig of coffee as Noah popped into the kitchen.

''Did you say please, Dad?''

Anthony's black eyes seared her. ''In my own special way I said pretty please. But it didn't work.''

Didn't work? Her whole body was boiling mush. She'd been on the verge. She was still wet. And hot. Burning up. Every nerve in her body was screaming for him. She wanted him so much. And the handsome snake knew it.

''You did this deliberately!'' she mouthed to Anthony.

''It was fun, wasn't it?''

A half sob bubbled up from her throat.

Then Noah looked up and began bouncing from one foot to the other. His eyes were so bright and intense, she swallowed the lump in her throat and tried to calm down.

"Please come," Noah whispered. "Please. Pretty please..."

"I tried to make her," his dad said with *that* smile.

Kill. "I really can't," she demurred.

Noah's eyes clouded with real pain. "He was mean, wasn't he?"

"Not exactly...."

"Not exactly?" Anthony winked at her.

"Then why?" Noah persisted.

"I just can't...."

"Make her come, Dad!"

"Believe me, I tried!"

"Just go—both of you!"

"All right. You win," Anthony said to her.

Why did she feel such loss as he stood up to go?

"But, Dad—"

Seven

Zoe was walking briskly along a narrow sidewalk in the bright sunshine past palm trees and tourist shops on her way to the bus stop. Determined to put Anthony out of her mind, she'd spent the past hour or two reading tour books on Rhodes. Not that she'd really been able to concentrate all that well on her reading. She could barely think about anything other than Anthony and their wonderful sex last night, and then their latest little adventure in the kitchen that had left her so restless and edgy.

Not that two hours would have been nearly enough time to read and understand about the Knights, who'd built their impressive fortress in Rhodes Town, even if she hadn't felt distracted by Anthony. What had those fighting monks who'd been so determined to fight Islam been about?

Motorcycles jammed the sidewalk in front of a

café, so she hopped down into the street to walk around them. The sun felt wonderful on her back and arms. Yes, she was definitely on her way into Rhodes Town to get her mind off sex. She was going to see the Knights' fort and think about ancient wars between Moslems and Christians instead of a certain handsome cowboy.

As she walked past a minivan, a motorcycle came out of nowhere and whipped past her so close she screamed. Dropping her books and purse, she tripped over them. Not that the rider looked back.

Picking her things up, she scrambled back onto her sidewalk as fast as she could, just as another motorcycle roared past her.

What was this thing Greeks had with motorcycles? They were such nice people—until they got on motorcycles. Didn't they have mothers to tell them that motorcycles were dangerous?

A horn tooted. Scared it was another motorcycle, she turned. A square, little red car she couldn't identify swerved as recklessly as the motorcyclist toward the curb beside her. She was about to scream when a brown, work-roughened hand that she most certainly could identify—hadn't it been all over her thighs just an hour or so ago in the kitchen—thrust the red door open.

"Sure, you won't go with us?" rumbled that deep, sexy drawl that made her homesick for Texas and turned her stomach to mush.

"No. Definitely. No. I'm not going with you." She spoke loudly and clearly even as she felt his gaze sear her naked legs.

Too bad she made the mistake of leaning down and meeting his burning gaze.

"You're blushing," he whispered.

She lost herself in the coal-bright depths of his eyes, which were deep and dark and spoke to her on some unfathomable, ungentlemanly level.

Noah's were white-hot with innocent eagerness. "Please, please, Aunt Zoe."

A tremulous silence hung over the three of them. She licked her lips. A dozen motorcycles roared past them.

"Don't go, girl. Sex last night. Then the kitchen..."

Much to everybody's surprise, especially hers, she ignored those worried little voices and slid a long bare leg inside the little car, slamming her door with a great deal of zest.

"Eyes on the road," she commanded saucily. "Oh, and by the way, where are we going?"

Anthony tried to hide his lopsided grin as he turned around and hit the accelerator.

"Dad! You know what the man said!"

"What man?" Zoe wanted to know.

"The man who rented Dad this car," Noah answered.

"The poor devil only owns three cars," Anthony explained. "He couldn't stop polishing the front bumper and the headlights even after he gave me the keys. He nearly wept when I put it in too high a gear as I drove off the lot. Yelled at me not to drive into *Rodos.*"

"What? That's where the Knights' fortress is. Where else would any self-respecting tourist want to go?"

"Exactly."

"He said not to park by rocks," Noah chirped from the front seat.

She leaned forward. "Why on earth not?"

"Because," Noah said, "the goats will jump on it."

They all laughed.

"Where are we going?" she asked.

"Lindos," Anthony replied.

Soon they were driving along the east side of the island where the cliffs were high and rocky and plunged to the sea. An hour or so later they reached Lindos, which was a white jewel of a village, its sun-drenched, boxy houses perched high above the sparkling, aqua sea on sheer rock ledges.

Anthony parked outside of town near rows of tour buses. The threesome headed down a steep, narrow road. They had to stay to the side to avoid dozens of motorcycles that zipped past them. When one roared too close, Zoe grabbed Noah's hand instinctively.

The little boy clasped her fingers tightly and looked up at her and smiled.

Her heart fluttered with strange longing when he held on to her so trustingly. He was so darling. And he needed a mother so much.

"I want one of those when I grow up," Noah said.

"A motorcycle? Do you remember that one-legged boy we saw in Athens?" Anthony countered.

"Don't scare him," Zoe whispered.

"I'm glad you came," Anthony said quietly when Noah loped ahead.

"I don't think I have a brain cell working."

He smiled. "Good. That's the way I like you."

She was dangerously glad she'd come to this charming town of small white houses that lined narrow, winding streets. But it wasn't being in Greece that was so wonderful. It was being with them.

She felt so alive and happy as they climbed past shops and vendors and tourists who spoke a babel of tongues, all the way to the ancient acropolis that crowned the village.

Sometimes Noah held her hand. Sometimes he rushed ahead. And always, always, she was too aware of Anthony at her side, the back of his hand lingering at her waist. It seemed he was constantly finding some excuse to touch her.

She knew she shouldn't be with them. She was here to forget Anthony. He belonged to the past. To Shady Lomas. To Rene. To scandal. Zoe had burned her bridges when she'd married Duncan. The whole town thought she was some sort of black widow or scarlet woman. She couldn't go back. She couldn't be in love with Anthony Duke…her nephew. Why was she even thinking about impossible possibilities?

The rocky path grew smooth and slippery. When Zoe paused in their climb to look at an embroidered tablecloth a woman had spread out on the rocks, she nearly stumbled. Instantly Anthony's dark hand was at her waist. Steadying her, he drew her closer to his own body.

His fingers burned through her sundress. As always, it was as if a jolt of electricity had passed through her. She jumped, startled.

Then his leg brushed hers. He stood so close she could smell him…his cologne…the laundry detergent that clung to his fresh, white dress shirt…and him…that clean male scent that was his alone. In one second she was back in the kitchen, her legs open, his mouth, his tongue…

Her palms grew damp. So did certain other unmentionable parts.

Oh, dear.

"Do you want the tablecloth?" Anthony's voice was a husky whisper against her ear.

"No." She bit her bottom lip. That wasn't what she wanted. She couldn't have what she wanted. She was the black widow, the shady lady of Shady Lomas. She'd become too rich, too unforgivably rich, when her older husband had died.

She'd loved Duncan at the end. Maybe not the way she'd loved Anthony. But then he hadn't hurt her the way Anthony had, either. Knowing that his death could happen at any moment, Duncan had been determined to live life to the fullest.

"I want all the old Goody Two-shoes to know I'm still kicking," Duncan had said one night. "And you and the stuffed-shirt-who-won't-own-me-as-his-uncle are too young and too serious to appreciate each other. People need to suffer a little before they marry. Mark my words. One day you'll be glad you married me."

Duncan hadn't made her crazy with jealousy and insecurities that drove her to— No, Duncan had been wise and understanding. In a strange way, he'd been the father she'd never had. But nobody wanted to hear that, least of all Anthony.

Well, all she knew was that there was no going back for either Anthony or herself. She belonged in Manhattan now. She was a big-city editor.

Right. You're like a scared little mouse in every editorial meeting. You dumped Veronica. Who are you without Veronica?

It was hot when they reached the ancient city. The

acropolis was crawling with sunburned tourists. Noah climbed up onto every rock and had to be watched and chased. Every time Noah looked at her or grabbed her hand, Zoe ached because she knew it was Rene he really wanted.

Rene belonged with them. Not her. Never her.

And yet…today the impossible felt almost possible.

Beneath them the windowpanes in the boxy, white houses caught the sun and shone like gold. Anthony came up to her.

"It's so beautiful here," she said to him.

He nodded, saying nothing, simply staring into her eyes. When the wind blew her hair into her face, he smoothed the tendrils back. Then he smiled. Her heart pounding, she turned away.

Later they found a roof garden with awnings to shade them and stunning views of the sea, acropolis and village. There was even a cat that looked sort of like Super Cat to throw scraps to. On the way home, Noah and she sat in the back seat and played adventure games. Then they opened the sunroof and stood up together, letting the wind blow through their hair as Anthony drove on the narrow, winding road.

The day was perfect. Unbearably perfect, and every perfect moment had made her want one more moment.

The little car raced through the two-lane streets of the last Greek village before reaching their suburb. The sun was low; the glowing light magical. And, oh, those misting, purple mountains in the distance, they were magical, too.

A few minutes later Tony pulled into the resort

parking lot. He cut the motor and smiled at her. She didn't know what to say.

"Thank you," she finally whispered.

"Thank you," he said.

He got out and opened her door. She put her hand in his. He helped her out, and together they gathered her things.

One day down and six more to go, she thought when they reached her door.

What about the nights? She couldn't stand it. She was head over heels in love with both father and son. Impulsive, impossible relationships were her specialty.

"What about dinner?" Anthony whispered against her ear.

"Tonight?" she squeaked.

"I've got that camp-out on the beach," Noah said, "with all the other resort kids. I can't eat supper with you."

"I know, son. I was asking Zoe for a date."

"Wow!" Noah's smile was so big, she saw every one of his new teeth. As he studied them both, his huge blue eyes became fever bright with eagerness.

"Of course, I…I should say no," she said.

"Neither one of us has been doing what we're supposed to lately," he murmured.

Remembering their interlude in the kitchen, she couldn't speak.

"Your place or mine?" Anthony whispered.

"Seven o'clock," she said. "My place."

Zoe was scared. Feelings of vulnerability had her shaking every time Anthony looked at her or got too close. The air in her kitchen seemed to sizzle, now that they were alone in it again—and there was nothing in the frying pan.

Dinner, which had been carryout Greek salad, roasted chicken and red wine was over. She and Anthony were seated across the table from each other again.

He glanced at his watch and then at her. "We have an hour and a half before camp-out ends. What do you want to do next?"

Her gaze left his handsome face and wandered around the room, avoiding *the* chair where he'd made her melt. "We could go for a walk on the beach."

"Yes." He got up from the table, stacked the dishes and put them in the sink. "We could."

"Noah loves all those perfect little rocks."

When she arose, he was right behind her.

"I'm not Noah." Anthony's hands touched her hair. Before she thought, she tilted her neck to gaze up at him. He took that as an invitation and slid his arms around her. His slightest touch held magic warmth and brought profound comfort and need. She felt his lips in her hair, and their heat burned all the way to her scalp and sent little shivers down her spine.

Oh, dear.

"How do I know you're not just after the ranch?" Her lips barely made a sound.

He cupped her breasts. "How do I know you're not just hot for my bod?"

"This is insane."

His hands moved lower, circling her waist. "Wildly so. Maybe that's why it's so much fun. I like the way you shake every time I touch you or look at you. The way you blush when I look at your legs.''

She liked it too. That was the trouble. ''Well, *I* don't. It makes me feel…'' Vulnerable and out-of-control…crazy with want to have the one thing I've been running from for years.

''My whole life has been about forgetting you,'' she said.

''Maybe we've both been on the wrong track. Do you know I've spent years and years working and taking care of people, doing what I'm supposed to. Years not giving in to any of my own feelings. I shouldn't have married Rene. I should have faced what I felt for you.''

''But you had the perfect marriage.''

''You can believe that myth if you want to.'' He paused. ''This week, when I first saw you, I was furious. So furious I began to realize I hadn't really felt much in years. Then I run into you in Athens and feel this powerful thing for you…. Why?''

''The black widow at work.''

''Don't call yourself that. What I'm trying to say is that you make me feel alive.''

''You've made me feel alive, too,'' she admitted. ''Why do you suppose that is?''

''Maybe it's just that you're dangerous and forbidden and I know I should know better than to trust you.''

''Ditto,'' she said, hardly daring to breathe.

''Or maybe…maybe we should stop analyzing it. Something tells me to just go for it. Let's see what happens…where this takes it. Let's find out why we feel the way we do. Life can get too predictable.''

''Not mine,'' she whispered.

He laughed. ‘‘I want to make love to you. But this time you have to admit, beforehand, that I’m not forcing you.’’

‘‘I’m supposed to be here thinking about my life. And…and writing.’’

‘‘Maybe being with me is the same thing. You’re living it. Your body is making up your mind for you.’’

She drew a breath to steady herself. ‘‘Not good.’’

‘‘Your body was always smarter than your brain, bookwormella.’’

‘‘Thanks a lot.’’

‘‘You’ve got a great body, and I’ve got a question.’’

She waited.

‘‘Do you want to finish what we started this morning in your kitchen?’’

‘‘What you started, not me.’’

‘‘There you go, blaming me—’’

‘‘Okay. Okay,’’ she admitted.

‘‘Well, do you—’’

‘‘Well, I’ll have to ask my great body.’’

‘‘What?’’

‘‘You said my body was smart.’’ She went to the kitchen counter and turned on the radio. Greek music filled the condo, and she began to sway back and forth to its beat.

‘‘What the hell are you doing?’’

‘‘You asked my body a question. It’s making up its mind. Does it or doesn’t it want to make love to you?’’

‘‘I’m waiting.’’

‘‘Just watch,’’ she whispered. Lowering the strap of her sundress, she whirled to the music. After a minute or two, her hand went for the zipper at the back of her dress. In the next instant the dress slid off her breasts, waist and hips to the floor, and all she had on was her black bra and black, lacy, thong panties.

She turned the music louder and began to undulate to the frenzied tempo. Soon the beat throbbed in every cell of her body. Or was it his narrowed, brilliant eyes that made her blood cells boogie?

She unhooked her bra. As her body swayed, her breasts bounced. Oh, man, the heat in his eyes and his obvious arousal when she threw her bra at him turned her on big-time.

When the music began to wind down, she danced her way to the bedroom. He followed. Last thing, she stripped off her panties and threw them at him, too. Then she bolted her door in his face.

He jiggled the knob. "Was that a yes or a no?" came his ragged voice.

"You tortured me this morning. Now it's my turn."

"Let me in, you sexy witch."

"The bod's thinking about it."

It didn't take the bod long. With shaking hands, she opened the door.

He stepped inside, her black thong panties dangling from a finger. He let them fall onto the white tiled floor. For a breathless eternity, their eyes devoured each other. Then he swept her in his arms. "Where did you learn to strip like that? What other tricks do you have up your sleeve?"

"No tricks. I just want you more than I can bear."

"Me, too." He slid his tongue into the honey-sweetness of her mouth, and she felt herself do a slow burn as he kissed her.

"I'm melting. I'm melting," she said.

"Me, too. Shut up. End of conversation. And..."

"And what?"

"No counting," he ordered.

"Okay," she whispered against his mouth. "But you have to promise to go slow and..."

"And?"

"And be tender."

"Tender? Like this?" When he traced the contours of her breasts with the tip of his tongue, she gave a long, drawn-out sigh of pure pleasure.

"You're off to a great start."

He began teasing her with little love bites on her throat and shoulders. Then he played with her hair the way he used to, winding it through his fingers and lifting it to his lips. "How beautiful you are."

"We're running out of time."

He drew her closer. "You said go slow and be tender."

"You promised to finish what you started this morning in the kitchen."

He made love to her sweetly and tenderly, satisfying her in every way. When it was over and she was nestled in his arms, feeling as limp and pliable and lazy as a well-simmered noodle, her telephone rang jarringly.

"Don't answer it," he whispered.

She picked it up. When the caller said hello and she recognized the voice, Zoe shot to a sitting position, her hands gripping the receiver like claws.

"Oh, dear." She let out a little moan of pure misery.

Anthony dove under the covers and put his tongue between her thighs.

Zoe gasped, "Who gave you this number?" Then she put her hand over the receiver and pushed at Anthony's broad warm shoulder.

But the distracting velvety tongue continued to flick and cause rapture. The voice on the other end of the line babbled frantically.

"Anthony, I can't concentrate." To the caller she said, "Up? You're here in Rhodes? Now?"

The tongue made thrillingly slow circling motions. In the next breath she shuddered in pure bliss.

"You can't come up! No!" she said to the caller. She patted Anthony's head, "Darling, you'd better go—now—"

"Who is it?" he demanded gruffly from under the sheet.

"I...I can't tell you! It's a secret! No! It's an emergency!"

He pushed the sheet out of the way and frowned at her. "Is it about Noah? Is he okay?"

Shaking her head, she cupped her hand over the receiver. "Go now, darling. I'll call you later."

"Is it a man?"

"Worse." She waved at him to go with her free hand. "Business. Please, just go."

He looked puzzled and a little worried as she pointed to his clothes and motioned to him to get dressed.

He stood up. "You're going to tell me what's going on—"

"Later." She nodded.

He was scowling as he pulled on his slacks. "Is it a man?" he demanded again.

"I already answered that question."

"You'd better be telling me the truth."

"I am. I swear."

"With our history, it's not so easy to trust you, you know."

"That was low."

He grabbed the rest of his clothes and stalked out of her condo.

"I'll call you," she cried.

With Anthony gone, Zoe lay back against her pillows and tried to give her full attention to her exasperating caller.

Eight

"Is someone else there?" Veronica was so overwrought her Texas drawl was way more pronounced than usual. The word *there* came out tha-a-a-a-re. "Did I call at a bad time?"

Oh, boy, did you? "Don't be ridiculous," Zoe said crossly. "This is a great time. What's wrong?"

"Is someone there?" Veronica demanded. "When I heard you were in Rhodes staying at some hideous time-share, I rented a villa on a mountain with olive groves and lemon trees that go down to the Aegean. It reminds me of Delphi."

"I haven't been to Delphi."

"Well, you should go. It's magical. The muse liked Delphi. Anyway, ancient history. I'm here. You can move into the villa with me...help me get this novel started.... It's called *Vanished.* This woman looks up her old boyfriend."

"You still hung up on the old-boyfriend theme?"

"Aren't we all? So, my characters have this big date, sort of a reunion. Sex. Everything is too perfect. Except…then she vanishes. Her twin sister gets worried and starts looking for her.

"The twin meets this man. Only I can't get started, and there's no spark. I keep writing the same sentence over and over."

"No. I cannot help you. Manhattan. Abdul. Super Cat—remember?"

"That dud. Not your cat—Abdul! He locked your precious cat in the closet and then he pounced at me in your hall. Honest! You're not going to let that worthless dud come between *us.* You know you're better off without him!"

"End of conversation." Zoe hung up on her.

The phone rang again. Only this time it was Anthony.

"What is going on?"

There was a loud knock at her front door.

"I really can't talk right now."

"Is this about a man?"

"No. Goodbye."

"Don't hang up—"

"Goodbye."

"Don't…"

"Sorry." Gently she placed the phone on the hook.

While Veronica pounded, Zoe took her time getting dressed. She found a pair of soft jeans and grabbed a white pullover cotton sweater out of a drawer. She even combed her hair and put on lipstick. And, of course, she had to make that bed. That took a while since all the sheets had come off and were in wadded tangles on the floor.

Only when the condo was immaculate did she open the door. Veronica's mouth fell open. "You...you look great! New nose? Or?"

Zoe fluffed her hair. "Same old me. But, hey, you look great too."

"How do you like my new boobs?"

Veronica bounced through the door in a skin-tight pink jersey top.

"Impressive. And you've gone back to blond."

Veronica shook her loose curls. "To go with my new movie-star figure. I'm having fun with it, too. This is definitely the real me."

"Okay. But after this, no more plastic surgery. Stop right there. Enough already."

"That's what my mother says. The nose is good. And the boobs are perfect. But she's always sending me pictures of these plastic surgery disasters. Faces of stars in tabloids who look like wax dolls melting."

"Your mom's right. No more surgery, okay? There's nothing wrong with you, Veronica. You are okay just as you are. Someday you are going to realize that."

"Since you dumped me, I'm into therapy." Veronica headed toward the kitchen. "Lots of dishes—" she whirled, and her voice went silky "—for a woman vacationing alone."

"Veronica, why did you come here?"

She whipped around. "You have to forgive me."

"I forgive you, but that doesn't mean I have to work with you. You betrayed me."

"Never again. You matter more to me than anybody...except my mother. I swear I'll never do anything to hurt you again. I was awful. I know. I wouldn't forgive me, but you're sweeter than me. And I'll go all to pieces if you don't."

"That is emotional blackmail."

"I know. I don't care how low I have to stoop to get you back. Just listen."

"Okay." Wearily Zoe went to the stove. "Hot tea?"

Veronica nodded, and Zoe set a kettle of water and lit a burner.

"In my defense, I was all alone in New York. I couldn't face Ursula or you without the ending of my book. But I couldn't write. What kind of writer misses all her deadlines? I had that huge advance—which I'd already spent. So much was riding on that ending. And then that creep wrote all those awful things on the Internet. I felt alone and desperate."

"You're repeating yourself."

"Okay. The point is I was just so crazy. The sex was awful. It made me really hate myself, and that was before you came in and found out. Please…please try to understand. I really am totally, truly, forever sorry."

Zoe couldn't help smiling. "As apologies go, yours is pretty inspired, but then you are a writer."

"I'm so sorry. Really—"

"All right," Zoe murmured as the teakettle whistled.

She poured tea. They both sweetened it.

"But you can't stay here now," Zoe said. "I have things going on in my own life. And I can't move in to your villa."

"But my book—"

"Hello?" Zoe took a long sip of hot tea and then

looked Veronica dead in the eye. "Are you listening? I have a life, too. I had an agenda of my own when I came to Rhodes."

"But...what about me—"

"We'll do a long lunch. Tomorrow. In Rhodes Town." Zoe grabbed a yellow guidebook off her stack on the table and thumbed through it until she came to a rooftop restaurant in the Knights' fortress she'd read about. "This place is supposed to be quiet, and it has lovely views. Bring your legal pads. We'll be inspired."

Veronica pulled out her address book and jotted the name of the restaurant down. "What would I do without you?"

"You'd be fine."

"Not without my muse."

She got up. They went to the door and hugged.

"I'm really glad to hear you're in therapy," Zoe said.

Zoe was dressed and needed to leave if she was going to be on time for lunch with Veronica, but Anthony wouldn't get off the phone.

"Why won't you tell me who this mystery lunch date is with?" Anthony demanded.

"I said I'll see you tonight."

"Lunch with this mystery person is going to take most of the morning and all afternoon?"

"I'll explain later."

"Is it a man?"

"No...for the fourteenth time!"

"Zoe—"

"Trust me."

"Trust Shady Lomas's black widow?"

"That's a low ball and you know it. How many times—"

"Sorry."

"That apology doesn't sound even a tiny bit sincere."

"Because it isn't."

"Because you're too macho and pigheaded."

"Any more of my flaws you'd like to list?"

"Oversexed."

"That's a flaw?"

"A fun flaw." Zoe glanced at her watch. "Look, I've got to go, or I'll be late for lunch."

"It's only ten."

"The person I'm meeting is extremely impatient."

"I want to meet this...this impatient person."

"And I want you to mind your own business."

"You are my business."

"One night of sex and you think you own me."

"Two nights and one morning. You know what they say about three being a charm."

"You don't own me, Tony."

"Zoe—"

"Goodbye."

"Zoe—"

"Take your mind off this. Play adventure games with Noah. And while you're at it, give him a kiss on his forehead for me."

"I'd rather give you a kiss somewhere else."

"Tonight. I can't wait." She blew him a kiss and hung the phone up slowly.

With Noah gone to resort camp again, Anthony couldn't contain himself. He had every window of the condo open, so he could smell roses and the salty

Aegean. But the lush setting only upset him and made him all the more edgy. Every time he thought about Zoe going to lunch with this mystery person in some romantic locale, he cursed silently. What was she pulling this time?

He stalked out to the patio and stared blindly at those infernal blue mountains across the aqua water. One minute he'd been kissing her between the legs and, damn it, she'd been melting, and then the next she'd sent him packing and all because somebody had called her. Would she tell him who? No! And now this mystery lunch date!

When they'd had hot sex as teens, Zoe had gotten neurotic about it and run off. When she'd caught Rene coming on to him, she'd believed the worst without even listening to him. Then the next thing he knew, she'd run off with Uncle Duncan and created the scandal of Shady Lomas.

Bookworm? Sexpot? Black widow? Who the hell was she? Had she and Uncle Duncan even had a real marriage?

Noah hardly knew her, but he already adored her. Like dogs, kids had highly honed instincts about human character. Kids hadn't been properly indoctrinated, so they saw through lots of bull. Thus, Anthony trusted Noah's instincts more than he did his own.

Bottom line—do you want the shady lady of Shady Lomas, who once utterly humiliated you, in your life…maybe forever?

Hadn't Aunt Peggy and his own mother set this up? They must think such a match was okay. Noah adored Zoe. Anthony adored her. Who else in Shady Lomas mattered?

So—who the hell was Zoe going to spend the day with when she should be with him?

"Trust me," she'd said.

Anthony did trust her. Well, sort of. He just had to know who she was with and where she was. When he heard her door open and close, he pulled back his window curtain just as she stepped out in a skimpy red sundress slit to the thigh. She was wearing strappy red sandals that made her legs look long and curvy.

Those legs. His legs. He had to follow those legs. Even as pride and indignation slammed full force into his conscience, he hid behind the curtain just long enough for her to disappear down the walk behind a tall green hedge. Then he grabbed his wallet and keys and raced after her.

"You have no right…"

"Damn it. I bedded her. She melts every time she looks at me. No matter what she's up to or who she's with, she's mine."

Anthony thought of the last nine years without her. They'd been dead, lonely years. Everybody but his mother had thought he was so happy with Rene, but he'd been living a lie.

He slid into his rental car when Zoe flagged a cab. When the taxi tore off, Tony turned his key in the ignition.

Nobody was taking her away from him again. Period. Because he loved her.

He loved her.

Anthony didn't have much time to reflect on that shocking thought. Nor did he want to. Her cab driver was a maniac. The madman ran lights, passed in no-passing zones. In the middle of Rhodes Town, Anthony got caught at a light and lost the jerk.

Anthony drove aimlessly for a while. Rhodes Town was so packed with tourists, it took him an hour even to find a parking place in a park under a palm tree. By then he felt so frustrated, he banged the steering wheel with both fists. Then he looked up at the colossal battlements, huge watchtowers and bridges of the Knights' fortress. Zoe was alone somewhere in that very romantic old fort with her mystery date.

Oh, God.... *Love?* He loved her? Such questions made Anthony feel like he was on a ship that was riddled with holes, a ship that was sinking really fast in a very deep ocean. He slid the key out of the ignition. He had to find her and start patching the holes in their relationship before they both drowned.

Real relationships weren't ever easy. But how could he possibly convince Zoe to leave her glamorous job in Manhattan and come back to him and face the narrow-minded people in Shady Lomas, who loved to gossip about her?

Determined to find her before she did something impulsive, Anthony got out of the car and started walking toward the magnificent golden walls of the old city. The Knights' fortified castle with its thick walls and wide mote filled with huge cannonballs was very impressive. If he hadn't felt so consumed with jealousy and uncertainty, he might have enjoyed stepping back into history.

If only Zoe had been at his side with Noah trailing along, he might have gladly paused to stare up at the high crenellated walls. He would have leaned against a low bridge and lifted Noah for a better view of all the cannonballs stacked up in little pyramids everywhere—in the mote, on the bridges, on the lawns.

The fortress was huge and made one think of the age of chivalry, of knights and armor. The Crusaders had been dead serious about not wanting Jerusalem to fall into Moslem hands. In a way that war was still going on.

Anthony trudged up the narrow, rocky streets for two hours, walked until his stomach was rumbling with hunger, and he felt crazy as hell.

Damn it! Where was she?

If she'd run off with another man…

Anthony imagined her in bed, melting beneath another man's lips, and rage and hurt shuddered through him.

"Trust me," she'd whispered.

He held on to that plea as if it were a lifeline and kept walking along the crenellated walls and stone towers.

He had to find her.

Nine

"You're really something!" Veronica said.

Veronica's golden hair was blowing about her naked shoulders. Voluptuous pink bosoms seemed to explode out of her tight green dress. "What are you—my spark plug!"

Zoe laughed. "I think I prefer the word *muse.*"

The rooftop Greek restaurant was as charming and as quiet as the guidebook had predicted. It had views of the marina and fortress. If Zoe stood, she could see the two bronze deer at the harbor's entrance.

Zoe had her usual Greek salad with a diet cola, so Veronica, who had a guilt complex about her voracious appetites, had dutifully followed suit.

They'd brainstormed an hour before lunch, and Veronica had written twenty pages of notes on her yellow pad. Instead of being scared and depressed, now she was excited about her book. Repeatedly she said she'd found her spark.

"You're a natural at dieting," Veronica said. "Me, I have to watch my figure."

"Which is spilling out of your chartreuse halter dress."

"After the surgery, I had to buy all new clothes. Or at least tops."

When Veronica polished off the last scraps of lettuce out of both their salad bowls, she called the waiter over and ordered more ouzo.

"You've had two glasses," Zoe reminded her.

"You're always counting. If I can't eat, I have to do something."

"I'm a counter." *Oh, dear.* For no reason at all, Zoe's mind turned to sex with Anthony that first night when she'd counted to prolong the ecstasy.

"Why, you're blushing," Veronica said. "Have you met somebody here?"

"If I were you, I'd watch the ouzo," Zoe cautioned in a dry tone. "It's too good."

"That sounds more like a recommendation than a warning." Veronica sipped the dregs from the glass the waiter had just set before her and then ordered another.

"It is and it isn't…a recommendation."

Zoe thought about her first night in Rhodes when she'd eaten alone and had drunk too much ouzo. Would she have fallen into bed with Anthony—the man she was supposed to be here to forget—jump-started if she hadn't been so mellow from ouzo?

Oh, well, that horse was out of the gate and galloping toward the finish line.

"I love him," Zoe whispered under her breath as she toyed with her fork.

"You're in lust."

"You're doing it. You're doing it."

"I want to *do* it with him tonight."

"That's not what I meant."

"You're talking to yourself again," Veronica said.

Zoe bit her lip and put down her fork. "Bad habit."

"And blushing!" Veronica said slyly. "I talk to myself all the time. That's how I start all my books. Then I start writing down what the voice says. I hate it when it stops talking." Veronica swirled her glass of ouzo. "I think this stuff is inspiring me. Or maybe it's just you—my muse. Hey! Back to the blushes. You didn't answer my question. Did you meet somebody?"

Zoe felt her cheeks heat again. "I told you I came over here to think…and to write a little."

"And have you written?"

"The same sentence over and over."

"I know that feeling. So, what have you been up to?"

Again heat crawled up Zoe's neck. "We're supposed to be working on *Vanished.*"

"You're blushing again."

"It's the sun."

"You're in the shade, love. And it's pretty cool out here with all these wonderful sea breezes."

"Rays are everywhere," Zoe siad. "I have a very delicate complexion."

"I know a blush when I see one. Who is he? Can I meet him?"

"After what happened in my apartment? Are you

crazy? Do you think I'd want you to meet any of my friends…if I had a man friend I mean."

"We're talking romance here. Not friendship. And it hurts me that you don't trust me."

"Veronica! We've discussed that until I'm sick of it."

"Okay. I know. It isn't an easy thing to forgive."

"What you did hurts more than what Abdul did. You really meant a lot to me. I went on the line for you. I had faith in you."

Veronica's face softened. She reached across the table and took Zoe's hand. "I'm very sorry about what happened in your apartment. You are so precious to me. I couldn't stop eating after I did that to you. I gained fifteen pounds in a week, and I've been on the most terrible diet ever since. I love you so much. I'm sorry. I swear I will never betray you again. Not even if you date Prince Charming!"

Zoe swallowed. "Okay. I think I'm starting to believe you, at least in this fleeting second. But trust takes time, understand? At least with me. You're not the only neurotic around, you know. I can be very jealous…when it comes to certain people."

"Your new boyfriend, you mean?"

Zoe nodded.

"I love you. I won't betray you again."

"So, let's get back to work. We only have a few more hours."

"And why is that? What are you doing tonight?"

"I have a life. Why is that concept so hard for you?"

"Boundaries? Right? My therapist is trying to drill that concept into me. All right. You have a life. No more questions. Work."

But while they brainstormed and scribbled on legal pads, Veronica kept watching her slyly and toying with her glass of ouzo. Like a bloodhound tracking a scent, Veronica couldn't let go. She was a writer and that made her too curious about people.

"I have to stretch," Veronica said. She got up and moved languidly over to the wall and looked down at the flagstone street.

Her face lit up. "Get up, Zoe! Have I got a sight for you!"

Zoe rose and moved toward Veronica.

"He's the one!" Veronica pointed down at a tall, broad-shouldered man in the street.

Anthony looked up as Veronica leaned over the wall, bosoms spilling out of her green dress as she waved to him wildly.

Zoe gulped. "But he's taken," she whispered. "He's mine."

Veronica didn't even hear her. Anthony waved back at her with equal lusty enthusiasm.

"Rene was blond and big on top," said a vicious little voice inside Zoe's head.

"You said if I was dating Prince Charming," Zoe whispered.

"Talk about Prince Charming. He's coming inside. Oh! Oh! He's coming upstairs. Oh! Where's my lipstick?"

"Veronica, there's something I've got to tell you—"

"Not now! I've got to go to the ladies' room and put myself together."

"Veronica, he's mine!"

Veronica had raced away. If she'd heard, she paid Zoe no attention.

So much for trust.

* * *

Anthony was so happy that Zoe was with a woman and not a man that he couldn't stop grinning at Veronica, who was a looker, if you went for the flashy, flirty type.

"My, my! So this is your long lunch date?" he asked Zoe.

"You two know each other?" Veronica wanted to know.

Anthony stared at Zoe. "You could say that."

"We have adjoining time-shares." Zoe's voice sounded dry. She felt as if she'd swallowed a lime whole and couldn't get it down.

"I asked her if she's met somebody here?"

"And what did she say?"

"Nothing. She didn't mention you at all. She used to have this boyfriend in Manhattan—Abdul. He looked a lot like you. I guess she goes for dark, handsome guys."

"Shhhh," Zoe growled at Veronica.

"I'm starving," Anthony said. "Do you mind if I join you?"

"Not at all," Veronica said in a thick, syrupy voice. She shot him a lush smile and leaned closer, pointing her pink bosoms at him.

He grinned again so broadly, Zoe wanted to slap him. "Stop slobbering," she whispered.

He arched an eyebrow her way. "Did you say something?"

"No!"

Veronica began to tell him that she was a big, important writer now but that Zoe had discovered her in the slush pile.

"For a long time she was the only person who believed in me," Veronica said. "Until I met Zoe, nobody ever thought I was much. Since I met her, I've been a star. But I've never written a book without her help. That's why I followed her here. I couldn't get my new novel started."

Anthony studied the thick legal pads. Maybe this woman had overdone the peroxide and the implants, but she was serious as hell about her work. So were a lot of people...like Zoe's boss. And Zoe herself. She'd run off from him in the middle of hot sex to deal with this blocked writer. That was really sweet of Zoe.

Anthony made up his mind that if Veronica was important to Zoe, he'd be nice to her even if it killed him. When Veronica put her hand on his knee and made a pass, he pushed her fingers away and smiled at both women awkwardly.

He had to be nice.

At some point Zoe bowed out of the conversation, so it was just him and the pushy blonde engaging in witty repartee. He finished lunch and said he had to go.

"No," Veronica pleaded. "This is just starting to get fun."

Zoe stood up. "We're through working, aren't we?"

"Oh, yes!" Veronica said. "This is definitely playtime."

Anthony was about to get up, too, but the hand with the long fingernails was back on his leg, clawing. If he sprang to his feet, he didn't trust what Veronica would do next. So he stayed put.

"Then I'm going," Zoe said.

"I've got my car," Anthony said. "Can I drive you back to the resort?"

"No. I'll get a cab. You two stay and enjoy yourselves."

"Zoe—"

"You two have fun!"

"Zoe!"

Zoe ignored him and ran toward the stairs. When he sprang to his feet, Veronica tackled him. By the time he'd gotten himself untangled and downstairs, Zoe's cab was speeding away.

The waiter came out and said, "Sir, your friend…the lady upstairs…that blonde…in the green dress…she's passed out."

Anthony raced back upstairs. Sure enough, Veronica was doubled over the table, blond hair spilling over the salad bowls and silverware. She was face-down in the breadbasket, her hand still gripping her last half-full glass of ouzo.

Five waiters circled him. When he glared at them, they shrugged their shoulders and looked up at the deep blue sky. Anthony cursed silently under his breath. He wanted to find Zoe, but Veronica was Zoe's most important writer. He couldn't just leave her here at the mercy of whoever found her.

Gently he shook her bare shoulder. "Veronica…"

At his touch, she muttered something incoherent. He lifted her head out of the breadbasket. Her lashes fluttered. She shot him a lush smile. Then she saw her waiter and waved her ouzo glass. "Empthy. Anotha-a…"

"You've had enough for one day, sweetheart," Anthony whispered, carefully lowering her head to the table.

"Get her downstairs," he said to the waiters. "I'll go get my car."

"And the check, sir?"

As Anthony slid his hand in his back pocket for his wallet, the biggest waiter leaned down and lifted Veronica over his shoulder. With her head hanging over his torso, her blond hair sweeping his knees, he carried her caveman style toward the stairs. She had a skinny waist, a big butt, long legs, not to mention incredible breasts.

She was a picture. But too loud and pushy. She didn't do it for him. Zoe did.

He had to take Veronica to her hotel and get back to Zoe.

When he returned to the restaurant in his red, rental car, the waiters placed a limp Veronica in the front seat. When they shut the door, she opened her eyes and gave Anthony a sexy smile that scared the hell out of him.

"What hotel?" he asked.

"Villa-a-a."

"Where?"

"Where do you want ith to be?"

"No games."

She laughed. Then she gave him another dopey smile.

"Where…"

"I heardth you," she lisped.

"You need to sober up."

Her sensual mouth curved. "I've got a better idea."

"Where is your villa?"

"I forgoth." Giggling, she put her hand on his leg.

He shoved her hand away. ''I'm serious about Zoe.''

She laughed as if this was deliciously amusing and leaned toward him—bosoms first.

''Thas what Abdul said.''

''Who the hell is Abdul?''

''Zoe's boyfriend.''

Ten

I swear I will never betray you again. Not even if you date Prince Charming!

Zoe picked up one of those perfect little round rocks that littered the beach and threw it as far as she could at the water. She should have sent Veronica packing.

When the rock she'd thrown vanished, she watched the water until it was smooth and glimmering like glass again. Then she threw another.

"How could you, Veronica? I told you he was mine."

But was he? That question made her chest hurt. With a savage flip of her wrist that made the little bones in her hand ache, Zoe sent another rock sailing high into the air. She watched the circle of ripples expand outward on the water.

How could he?

With a vengeance, Zoe whispered every bad word in her vocabulary. Some of the expressions were so gross, she smiled. Her repertoire was pretty awesome. She read a lot. Some of her writers could get colorful.

Not that the cussing or the rock throwing helped much. Zoe was upset with both Anthony and Veronica, but *his* betrayal hurt the worst. She remembered losing him to the beautiful, perfect Rene, who'd told Zoe so often she wouldn't be able to hold on to him. Was that still true?

And how dare Anthony follow her to the restaurant today! How dare he flirt when Veronica had thrown herself at him? Couldn't he see how mixed-up and vulnerable Veronica was? She didn't know who she was, much less what she wanted.

"How can you be worrying about Veronica? She's the other woman."

"You're doing it."

"I always talk to myself when I'm crazy and out of control."

Furious and hurt, Zoe sat down on the beach. As the sun sank and the air got cooler, she huddled beneath a towel some tourist had forgotten, her gaze fixed on those magical mountains across the sea. Slowly they went from gray to violet and then to glowing orange as the sun plopped into a hot-pink sea.

And still no Anthony.

When it was dark enough for the stars to pop out in little pinpricks of brilliance through the velvet blackness, she wrapped the towel around her and slunk back to her condo like a wounded animal.

In her kitchen she walked past her fruit bowl and

fridge without glancing at them. It was way past the dinner hour, but she was in too much pain to feel hunger.

Alone in her bedroom she sat down at her desk and faced her empty yellow legal pad. She lifted a pen, uncapped it and then stared at her pale reflection in the mirror. Not that she really saw the glazed brown eyes or her lank, windblown hair.

No, she was back under that arbor on the rooftop in the middle of the Knights' fortress. Veronica's lush bosoms were bobbing up and down like apples in a barrel, and Anthony's grin was growing bolder and whiter every time she jiggled them.

"You're wallowing."

"You're doing it."

Zoe chewed the tip of her pen. Then she bent over the yellow pad and began to write. Words flowed in scrawls of black ink as she spilled her raw pain onto paper. An hour or so later when she was done, she felt a little better, but when she read the first sentence, she was so horrified by her maudlin dribble, she nearly got sick.

Why had she ever thought she could be a writer? She was an editor. She never came close to really expressing what was in her heart the way Veronica could. Zoe was in awe of people like Veronica. That's why she'd let Veronica run over her. Veronica was this megatalent, this big author.

"But as a person, she's so fragile and lost, and she's a miserable human being. The slightest little thing reduces her to less than nothing."

"She got your man, though."

"The new va-vooms got him."

"The only man you ever loved was positively drooling over them."

Zoe ripped the pages out of her tablet, wadded them into a tight yellow ball which she pitched into her trash can. Then she just sat there, staring at herself for an endless time until the phone rang.

Anthony? She hated herself for feeling the slightest bit of hope. Then she dived across her bed to get it.

A lady with a British accent said, "Your nephew called and said he was in a bit of a jam."

"Who is this?"

"Bridget—at the front desk."

"Right."

"Seems Mr. Duke can't get back to pick up his son from our camp on time. He asked us to call you—"

Zoe repeated some of her most colorful expletives under her breath. *The jerk didn't have the nerve to call her himself.* "Of course, I'll come get Noah—"

Noah was waiting for her just inside the resort camp gate clutching three drawings, his lunch box and his electronic game. "Where's Dad?"

"Out with a friend."

"Who? You're his only friend here."

"He made a new friend today."

"Who?"

"Hey!" she whispered, determined to distract him. "What are these pictures?"

"We went to a taverna. I drew fishing boats." Noah was not to be distracted. "When's Dad—"

"He'll be here soon. What did you do at camp all day?"

He told her with immense, highly animated detail,

his hands waving as he spoke. He'd met a biker from Germany at the taverna, who smoked a lot of cigarettes and wore a black bandanna. The children had gone to the ruins of Kamiros, the smallest of the three ancient cities on the island of Rhodes.

"Zoe! There were all these tiny rooms with no roofs. What happened to the roofs? How did dirt get in the houses? Where's all their chairs and tables and beds? Would the roofs come off our houses? Will our houses fill up with dirt someday? Where did all their furniture go?"

She laughed. "So many questions." She thought for a moment. "I'm not really an archeologist, but I think houses made of stone are better preserved than the kind we live in now."

He listened as she tried to answer him. When she was done, his blue eyes grew laser bright. "Who?"

"Who?" Zoe played stupid.

The bright eyes refused to look away.

"What?" she whispered.

"Who's he with? How come Dad isn't with us? How come you won't tell me why? How come you look sad? Is he—"

"Oh, Noah…Noah…" She wrapped him in her arms.

He shuddered and drew away. He paled and seemed to grow smaller. Then his cheeks flushed cherry bright. She'd frightened him. He was remembering Rene and worrying that his father might be dead, too.

"He's okay. Nothing's happened…. Noah, your dad's fine."

"Really? Nobody would tell me about Mother at

first. They just looked at me funny the way you're looking at me.''

''Really?'' She pulled him into her arms again, and they snuggled close. Her fingers brushed his hair back from his hot brow. Nobody had told her about her parents' death for a while either.

''Why would he go out with somebody else when you're here?''

''Oh, Noah.'' She hugged him even tighter. ''Let's not worry about him anymore. Let's just have fun.''

''Like, can we play some games?''

''You bet. And for as long as you like—''

''Oh, boy.'' He dug in his backpack for his electronic game.

They had dinner together at her kitchen table. Then they played games until Noah's bedtime.

''You're not very good at this,'' he said, yawning sleepily after she'd lost a fourth game.

It had been hard for her to concentrate. ''Maybe you're just very, very good,'' she said.

''Really?''

''You're a champ.''

She gave him a glass of milk and boiled her toothbrush so he could use it to brush his teeth. He took off his clothes and she loaned him one of her big T-shirts. When he was dressed for bed, she tucked him beneath the sheets and blanket and tried not to remember that this was the same bed where Anthony and she had made passionate love only last night.

She sat down by the bed in the dark and tried not to think about Anthony at all as the clock on the dresser ticked mercilessly.

She hugged herself and tried not to imagine Anthony in Veronica's bed. Of course, her overactive imagination refused to cooperate. Visions of Anthony and Veronica rolling over and over on a Turkish rug in a luxurious villa bedroom with views of olive groves that went down to the Aegean danced in Zoe's brain. Soon she was half-crazed with jealousy. And still the clock ticked relentlessly.

At midnight her doorbell rang.

Zoe ran to the door and stared through her peephole. The curve of the little glass distorted her view. Anthony and the golden woman hanging from his arms looked like two fat dwarfs captured in a weird, glass bubble.

"Don't open it," warned a voice.

Zoe flung the door open. "Good evening, Anthony," she said.

Their gazes locked. She saw the dark circles beneath his black eyes and read his silent plea for help and understanding. His shoulders drooped. He looked as if he'd been in a fight or worse. Instinctively, Zoe's heart melted with sympathy for him. Then the visions of the couple on the Turkish rug started dancing, and her heart iced over.

"Now I understand why you were so upset last night when she called," he said. "You'll never believe the stunts she pulled."

"Try me," Zoe whispered in a faint, tortured voice.

"It's late. You don't want to know."

She nodded. "You're right."

Even in this moment of utter betrayal, Zoe wanted him. Even though he held a half-naked woman in his arms, a woman who was her protégé and friend, even though visions of them making love cavorted in her mind, Zoe still ached to be in his arms.

"Fool."

"You're doing it."

She bit her tongue and bent her head so he couldn't see the raw need in her face. Stepping back from the door, she let him pass.

"Noah's in my bed. You can put her on the couch," Zoe said crisply.

Zoe held her head high and tried not to show the slightest sign of her true feelings as he carried Veronica inside. None of the shock, none of her exquisite hurt must he see. Yes, even these moments when he held another woman, even these fresh insults had to be endured with no sign of the pain she felt. She was not going to let him humiliate her again and make her do something impulsive and crazy.

He laid Veronica down on the couch. Then he pulled a pair of green high heels, a bra, and shiny green thong panties out of his pocket. He placed the shoes on the floor beside the couch and stuffed the underwear into them.

Oh, dear. The visions started dancing again. Only this time the costumes were different. The woman underneath Anthony rolling on the carpet wore nothing but green thong panties.

Zoe rushed to the shoes and yanked out the thong panties and waved them at him.

His dark face was contrite and embarrassed. "Your friend is…is…confused."

"P-please—"

Zoe waved the thong panties wildly. He grabbed them. For a ridiculous moment, they played tug of war. Then she let go, and they popped into his brown hand.

"They're yours," she spat. "You earned them."

"What?" He stared at her, reading her too easily. "You think I—"

"I have eyes."

"I guess it looks bad," he admitted.

"She took off her clothes, didn't she? She attacked you, you'll probably say."

"Worse."

"You surrendered...after a long battle?"

"How dare you say that? You know her. And you know me."

"And I know what I see."

"Listen to me, Zoe. I love you."

"Love? You must think I'm a pea-brained idiot."

"I love you," he repeated.

"Don't say that!"

"I—"

"I don't care."

"You don't mean that," he whispered.

"I don't want the man I marry to sleep with a friend of mine and then say he loves me. That makes me feel crazy. And I've spent enough of my life feeling crazy about you."

"You have?"

"Nine impossible years. Not to mention when we were kids."

"You've been crazy about me while you were in Manhattan?"

"Yes! Yes! Yes!" She threw up her hands in disgust. "Well, no more. I came here to get over you. And now I have. We're through. I was a dumb, innocent girl the first time. I loved you so deeply. I hurt so much."

"You hurt? I can tell you about hurt. And about

guilt—'' The scorn and anguish in his voice made her heart tighten.

''I married Rene, a woman I didn't love, to get even because you'd made me the laughingstock of the whole damned town. You'd married my uncle Duncan. I thought people would stop laughing if I married Rene. And you know what, they did.''

''Oh!''

''But I paid a hellish price. I never loved her. I married her because she was your best friend. I made her miserable. Oh, I tried to be a good husband. I tried to love her. But trying wasn't good enough for either one of us. Without love, she sort of withered. She put on weight, let herself go. Then she got sick. I know everybody said I nursed her faithfully at the end. But I owed her a lot more than that. She knew it and I knew it. She was my son's mother and a wonderful mother, too, but behind closed doors, where it really counts, our marriage was hell. We stopped sleeping together years ago. She'd asked me for a divorce right before she got sick. Then we got the diagnosis, and I swore I'd take care of her. She agreed because she wanted to be with Noah as much as possible. I haven't told anybody any of this but you.''

''Oh…I'm…sorry.''

''Apparently, she'd always loved me, so I really hurt her. She was a wonderful cook…sweet… maternal… Rene would have made some man a perfect wife. But not me. Because of you, you little fool. I loved you then, and I love you now.''

''What about Veronica?''

''What about me?'' Veronica said, yawning, sitting up like a cat getting to her haunches. She ran her hands through her wildly tangled hair.

The hands froze in midair when she saw Zoe. "Oh, no, no! Not again." She turned on Anthony. "I told you not to tell her about us. She's my muse. I need her. I told you she's insanely jealous."

"I don't care what you told him," Zoe said firmly. "Get your high heels and your damned thong panties and your fake va-vooms back to your own villa. Write your own darn books from now on."

"But I can't!"

"You should have thought about that before you made love to Anthony on that Turkish rug."

"What Turkish rug?" Anthony demanded.

"The rug doesn't matter! Out! Both of you!"

"But nothing happened," Anthony said.

Zoe went to her door and slung it open for them.

"You have to believe me," he said.

The door banged against the stopper. "I don't have to…to anything." Zoe drew a breath. "Oh, you'd better get Noah. He's asleep on my bed."

When Veronica and Anthony and Noah finally left together, Zoe resisted the impulse to slam the door. Because of Noah she shut it very gently, but when she got to her bedroom she began throwing all her makeup and clothes at her backpack.

"What are you doing?" the voices began.

"Packing! Shut up and leave me alone!"

"You're doing it. You're doing it."

The phone rang.

"For what it's worth, I love you," Anthony said softly.

She took a deep, agonized breath. "When my parents died, I hurt so bad for so long, I went numb. I never wanted to love you again because I never wanted to feel like that again. I don't want to marry you. I just want to feel numb again. Don't call anymore."

She slammed the phone down.

Eleven

Even at this early hour, the Greek sun was dazzling.

Zoe tapped her room key against the counter in the lobby. ''Hello? Somebody? I need to check out!''

A slim woman in a burgundy-colored suit with a gold pin that said Bridget came out of a back office and smiled at her. When Zoe returned the smile, her lips froze.

The young woman wore wire-rimmed glasses and had her blond hair pulled on the top of her head in a Tinkerbell knot.

''That was some hot date your nephew had last night,'' the clerk said in a beautiful British accent.

''Do you take Visa, Bridget?'' Zoe's voice was crisp as she snapped her credit card onto the polished mahogany and then shoved it toward her.

As Bridget zipped the card through her scanner, she looked almost wistful. ''When your nephew barreled into the parking lot, his date was standing up in the back seat. That little window in the top of his car was open.''

''You mean the sunroof?''

Bridget nodded. ''Well, she was topless. Her blond hair was blowing and she was having a lovely time waving her arms at the sky. I was afraid somebody would see them and call the police and get your nephew arrested.''

''If I'd seen them, I would have made the call myself.''

The clerk shot her an odd look as she printed Zoe's bill and handed it to her. Without a word Zoe signed it. Slinging her backpack over her shoulder, she raced out to the little side street behind the resort to hail a taxi.

A yellow cab rushed up just as Noah came running up to her. ''Wait! Wait! We're leaving, too! Do you have room for us, too?''

Zoe knelt, and Noah came flying into her arms. ''Not today, my precious darling.'' She stroked his straight hair and stared into his eyes, trying to memorize everything about him. Big teeth. Bright blue eyes. Spiky yellow hair. Freckles.

''Oh, Noah.'' She hugged him closer.

He put his head on her shoulder and clung. ''Are you leaving because Dad made that new friend?''

She swallowed a deep breath.

Gently he pushed away so he could see her. ''Is that why?''

Intense longing filled her as she studied him. He was wearing overlarge beige shorts and a white T-shirt and his tattered sandals. A half-eaten edible necklace of brightly colored candies hung from his neck. In one hand he gripped two small stuffed animals and a yellow paper.

''What do you have in your hand?''

''Beanie Babies and a paper I found in your trash can. Were you writing a story?''

''Oh, dear.'' He had that awful note when she'd spilled out her heart last night. ''That's my paper. Could I have it?''

His eyes danced with mischief as he wadded the paper tighter and hid it behind his back. She was about to plead with Noah to hand it over, when Anthony stepped out of the resort with their suitcases.

Instantly she forgot all about her crazy scribbling. She had to get out of here—fast.

''Goodbye, Noah.'' She hugged him.

When she stood up, Anthony yelled for her to wait. She pressed Noah's fingers and then touched his cheek. ''Goodbye,'' she repeated. ''I won't ever forget you.''

Noah's eyes glistened. ''Hey! You can have one of my lucky rocks.'' His cheeks paled as he slipped a perfect round rock into her hand.

''Thank you,'' she whispered.

Quite suddenly he began to cry.

''Oh, darling, darling, don't.'' She knelt again. ''I wish I could stay, but I can't.''

''You could. You can do anything you want to do. That's what Nana says.''

''No, Noah.''

Then she got in the cab and told the driver she was in a hurry to make her plane. She clutched Noah's rock tightly against her heart as her cab sped away just as Anthony raced out to the curb and yelled at her to wait.

* * *

Zoe had a window seat on her return flight to Athens. A plump little old lady with blue hair had the aisle seat. The middle seat was empty.

Suddenly a little boy in beige squirmed across the old lady's knees and threw himself into the middle seat.

"Looks like we've got the same seat assignment problem again," said a deep male voice bristling with tension.

"We can play a game together as soon as I finish this one," Noah said to Zoe.

Zoe barely glanced up at Anthony. "Go away and leave me alone," she whispered. Then she tugged at the twin halves of her seat belt and snapped them together.

"Not until you let me explain."

"I can fill in the dots, thank you very much. Veronica was riding around half-naked in your car. Her thong panties and bra were in your pocket."

The blue-haired lady sucked in a deep breath. "Thong—" Her head bobbed as she turned from Anthony to Zoe.

Noah's head was bent low over his game. Thank goodness, he was totally absorbed.

"Veronica's idea," said Anthony in a low voice. "Not mine."

"And you loved every minute of it."

"What the hell was I supposed to do with her? She was *your* important writer."

"Not anymore!"

"Oh, blame me for that, why don't you?"

"You tempted her to betray me again."

"Again?"

"Never mind."

"You introduced us. You could have told me what she was like the night before."

"I didn't trust you. And with good reason. You followed us. Then you fell for her like a ton of bricks."

"This is ridiculous."

"Right. So go!"

Passengers and luggage stacked up fast behind Anthony. When the flight attendant shoved her way through the throng to settle the dispute between Anthony and Zoe, she took their boarding assignments and counted passengers and seats. Then she recounted and then recounted a third time.

When she returned with their boarding passes, she was white with tension.

"Sir," she said, handing Anthony his boarding passes. "I'm very sorry, but we don't have enough seats."

"But I have two valid passes."

"But we only have one seat left on the plane. You and your son need two seats."

"I'll sit with Aunt Zoe," Noah volunteered cheerily, looking up from his game. "Dad, you can take the next plane."

"But I'm going to New York, darling," Zoe said.

"So are we," Noah countered.

"What?" Zoe glanced at Anthony warily. "Don't you dare follow me to New York."

"If you won't listen to me here, you leave me no choice. We have to talk."

"There's nothing to say. I won't see you. Understand? We've been through all this. It's finished."

"Sir...sir," the flight attendant said. "You really must get off the plane."

"All right. I'm getting off, and you're getting off too, young man." Anthony placed a hand on Noah's lap and undid his seatbelt. "Have it your way, Zoe. You win this round."

"You could get off, too, Aunt Zoe, and come with us—"

"I'm afraid I can't—"

"Aunt Zoe—"

"Quit calling her that," Anthony snapped. "She's not really your aunt, damn it."

"You said she was!"

"I just said it to make her mad."

"If you'd be nice and say you're sorry, maybe she'd get off, too."

"Noah! We've got to go!"

With a broad hand still on Noah's shoulder, Anthony herded Noah, whose blond head kept whipping around to see if Zoe would change her mind at the last minute and follow them down the aisle.

She didn't.

The last thing Zoe saw as the plane taxied down the runway was Noah clinging to a chain-link fence waving at the plane.

She put her hands on the glass. Condensation dripped across the little window like tears.

Father and son blurred.

"Cute kid," the old lady said. "Precious."

"Yes!"

"And the man's as handsome as the devil."

"Great analogy." Zoe opened her paperback and pretended to read. But the words ran together. Her mind was too muddled to read. All she could do was sit there.

It was a long flight home.

Zoe stepped into her apartment and Super Cat appeared and began rubbing against her legs. She went to her bedroom and flung her backpack down on the bed and unzipped it. Super Cat hopped inside and began sniffing the bag and her clothes in an attempt to fathom where she'd been.

Liking the scent of her green sundress, he lay down on top of it, slitted his eyes at Zoe and began flicking his tail, daring her to disturb him by trying to slide something out from underneath him.

"I guess I'd better go open your tuna or I'll never get unpacked."

Jade-green eyes blinked at her. Then Super Cat yawned and laid his head on his two front paws.

"Stubborn!"

She was staring out her window at her view of multitiered rooftops when her doorbell rang.

"Now, who could that be?" Her heart racing, she dashed down the hall. When she stared through the peephole, Abdul was squaring his shoulders and adjusting his tie. When she threw the first bolt, he thrust out his chin. He looked wonderful. He had on that single-breasted suit made of worsted blue wool he'd had custom made in London last fall. He only wore it for the most special occasions.

When she opened the door, he stepped inside carrying a bouquet of red roses and a black velvet jewelry box.

"What's the occasion?" she asked.

"No occasion. I just remember you had those pictures in your hall that needed hanging. Your apartment's old. High ceilings. And I'm tall.'' He smiled sweetly at her.

Men were so hopeful.

He handed her the bouquet.

''Thank you. Roses. My favorite,'' she said.

If you don't count bluebonnets.

She lifted the flowers to her nose and inhaled their fragrance. ''They're beautiful. I'll find a vase. And how very helpful of you to remember about the pictures.''

''It's the least I could do. I promised I'd do it, didn't I.''

''Months ago.''

She got out a stool and held the hammer and nails while he hung the photographs, which were all of Super Cat in cute poses. When Abdul secured the last three over her bookshelf, she made them jasmine tea.

''So, how was Rhodes?'' he asked, squeezing lemon into his cup.

She sipped, but her tea was too hot. So she set her cup down before she burned herself. ''I found out I belong here.''

''Bad vacation?''

''Rhodes was lovely, but I don't really want to talk about it.''

The doorbell rang before they'd finished their tea. She looked up, startled.

''You expecting someone?''

''No. I'm home an hour, and suddenly it's like Grand Central Station.''

''Everybody missed you. At least, I did.''

Suddenly it was a relief not to face Abdul and that

little black box, a relief to have an excuse to answer the door.

She got up. Once again she glanced through her peephole.

"Noah! Anthony!" she said, opening the door.

Noah raced inside, but Anthony stopped abruptly when he saw Abdul and Abdul's flowers and the black velvet box on the table beside their empty teacups.

"Who's this?" Abdul demanded, rising as if he still had the right to ask.

"Who's he?" Anthony's dark voice held equal, proprietary displeasure.

"I'm her boyfriend, that's who," Abdul said. "Who are you?"

"Her boyfriend? Since when?"

"Since a year ago."

Anthony's eyes locked on Zoe's pale face, willing her to say Abdul was lying.

But she nodded. "I did tell you not to follow me here."

"What was I?" Anthony ground out. "What was Rhodes?"

"What was Veronica to you?" Zoe asked.

"Nothing! That's what I keep trying to tell you!"

"There! What was Rhodes, you ask. I'll give you the same answer you gave me—nothing." She moved toward the door and pushed it wider. "Please go."

"Okay. I get it. Noah, come here—"

"But we just got here, Dad, and she's got this cool, fat cat." He broke off sneezing.

"Leave the cat alone. You're allergic. He might bite—"

"He won't bite," Zoe retorted touchily, defending Super Cat. "He has a wonderful disposition."

Anthony turned from Noah to her. "One last thing," he said as Noah knelt to pet Super Cat, "before I go..."

"Just leave."

Before Zoe knew what happened, Anthony took a long step toward her and spun her around roughly in his arms. For an eternity his mouth hovered an inch above hers. Then he pushed her against the wall.

"Don't," she pleaded, even as her heart pounded wildly and quite eagerly against her rib cage.

"I love you, you little fool," he whispered. "Doesn't that matter?"

Stubbornly she shook her head back and forth. "Not if you lie and cheat."

"Damn you. You're always assuming the worst about me. About yourself, too. You didn't ever believe we belonged together when we were kids. You thought you were this geek. You were a doll—precious, smart, sweet. I loved you, but you wouldn't let yourself believe it."

"You went from me to Rene."

"No, I didn't. You thought I did, so you married my uncle. Then I was an idiot to marry her so impulsively. I made her miserable because I loved you. But what's the use? You're so insecure, you probably prefer to believe the bad stuff." He snugged her closer. Then he lowered his mouth and rained hard kisses on her face and her cheek and the lush curve of her ivory throat with a desperate passion.

She fought him, pushing at his shoulders even as his arms tightened around her rigid body. His urgent kisses aroused feelings she didn't want, feelings and truths that wouldn't stop until he let her go.

"You humiliated me in Rhodes and you'll do it again," she said. "So you can't be here! And you can't do this! We can't do this!"

"*Please,* Zoe. I came here to ask you to marry me. The three of us could hop a plane to Vegas and be married today."

"I don't want to marry you."

His tongue slid against her lips, and Zoe let out a breathy moan. "I'm getting over you if it's the last thing I do."

"That so?" The pain in his eyes tore a hole in her heart even before he kissed her again, tenderly this time and with so much love, she melted utterly.

Only she didn't tell him she loved him nor did she even kiss him back. She'd never be able to hold on to him. She knew that now. There'd always be a Rene or a Veronica.

When he released her, she stood still against the wall, her head turned away from him.

"Marry me," he whispered.

"No." She kept her eyes downcast until he and Noah trooped outside.

"Who the hell was that?" Abdul demanded in a surly tone from his chair when they had gone.

She sighed. She'd totally forgotten Abdul was there. "You, too, Abdul."

"What?"

"Just go."

"Me?"

"You. And take that little black jewelry box."

"But you don't even know what's inside it."

She lifted it and placed it in his hand. "I know

enough. I know we don't belong together. I...I think I only dated you because you looked like him."

"The caveman who was just here with the kid?"

She sighed. "You're a nice man. Find some nice girl. Have a nice life."

"What are you going to do?"

"I haven't a clue. I need some time alone...to think."

"But..."

"Veronica wasn't the first girl, was she?"

"You and I weren't married. You were always so busy."

"Always reading," she agreed. "Always so upset about things that went on at work."

"And that crazy writer. You didn't pay nearly enough attention to me."

"Then go find that nice girl who will." Zoe's voice was gentle.

"The caveman had a point about you not believing in yourself. You should listen to him. I used to tell you the same thing."

"The last thing I need is advice from you."

"You should try listening."

She touched his arm. "Goodbye."

They hugged one last time. Then he left, and she was alone.

Her mouth burned from Anthony's kisses. Her heart ached for more, but the intense longing she felt just made her more determined than ever to forget Anthony Duke.

Vegas? He'd asked her to marry him. He'd said he loved her.

She touched her bruised lips. "I love you, too," she whispered, and then, determined not to cry, she brushed at the hot tears that stung her eyes.

Twelve

Sweat dripped off the end of Anthony's straight brown nose as he stubbornly eyed the wild-eyed palomino in the center of the round corral.

"You're not getting up on that horse again," Henrietta said. "I won't stand here and watch my only son commit suicide."

"Then go inside." Anthony wiped his brow and then leaned back against the wooden fencing.

"Don't you be sassing me."

Anthony bit his tongue to keep from saying anything. Ever since he'd come home from Rhodes, he'd been madder than hell at his mother for setting him up with Zoe.

"How come you can't ride 'im, Dad?" Noah wanted to know. "You said you could ride anything."

"Damn it, I can."

The palomino laid both ears back at the sound of Anthony's voice.

"You ain't been yourself, boss, since you got back." Frank, his top hand, spit a wad of tobacco onto the ground near Anthony's boots. "Your timin's off."

Going through the motions. That's all Anthony had been doing since he'd come home from New York. Without Zoe, his whole damn life was off, and there wasn't a damn thing he could do about it but go on living and hoping, making it through the days and the hellish nights.

"You've got better things to do than ride that bronc," Henrietta said. "You should be in the breeding barns or revising those new hunting leases."

She was right, of course. Besides running cattle, Anthony was a scientific deer breeder. He used stud stock to improve the breed and sold the progeny to high-fence ranchers in Texas, who could charge more for their deer leases if hunters walked away with trophy kills.

But the wild ride on the bronc in the corral resulting in aches and pains took his mind off losing Zoe. Not that Anthony could admit his heartbreak or how bleak his future seemed. Not to anybody. The trick to life was to ignore pain and go on.

He jammed his Stetson onto his brow and made a beeline for the thick braided-cotton reins trailing beside the palomino. To his surprise, the beast stood still when Anthony came up to him and eased his pointed black toe into the stirrup. Then Anthony grabbed hold of the horn and quickly swung himself up in the saddle. In another minute he had his other boot in the stirrup.

The palomino just stood there.

''Don't just sit there like a damn sissy, boss!''

''You shut your mouth, Frank,'' Henrietta warned.

''Ride him, Dad!''

Anthony turned his boot toes out and nudged the palomino gently. That set him off. The palomino went wild. He began to buck, lunging upward, crashing down. Again and again, the palomino hit the ground with bone-rattling thuds.

''You got 'im,'' Frank yelled.

The trouble with Frank was he was too damned optimistic, and his optimism always jinxed things. Sure enough, in the next second the palomino threw his damn head down.

''Pull his head up, boss.''

''Easier said than done,'' Anthony fumed.

Anthony pulled with both hands on those reins, but the horse was powerful in his brute strength. He jumped high, kicking all the way down again and again until Anthony hurt all over. Which was good because only then could he forget *her.*

Then Frank started cussing up a storm, and Anthony flew out of the saddle, flying higher than the tops of the stunted mesquite trees and swearing even louder than Frank.

Then Anthony hit the ground hard, scraping his chin and jaw on a rock. But the pain almost felt good 'cause it hurt so bad he stopped thinking about her.

It was raining lightly outside the offices of Field and Curtis. There was no wind, and the black wall of buildings across the street seemed to be holding up the heavy, dark sky.

Zoe hated these steamy, spring days.

"You've got to talk to Veronica," Ursula said.

"I'm not her editor."

When Ursula arched her brows, Zoe crossed her arms and hoped Ursula couldn't feel her panic slipping out around the edges.

Ursula was always so suave, so sure of herself. Today her black bob was as glossy as ink, and, as usual, not a single hair was out of place. She was wearing high-heeled navy pumps and a navy silk suit.

Zoe felt very unattractive by comparison in her rumpled slacks and a cotton sweater. She had stuck a red pencil into the messy knot at her nape when she'd been editing a manuscript and forgotten it was there.

"Believe me, I wouldn't ask you to do this if I had any other options. We've all tried to work with Veronica. She's..."

"Impossible," Zoe supplied.

"You and she have a special chemistry."

"I used to think so."

Zoe stared past Ursula at the skyscraper cliffs and the park in the misty, dreary distance. Why had working in New York seemed so glamorous? It felt empty and wrong, not the right life for her at all somehow.

"What really happened in Rhodes?" Ursula asked, her voice softening.

The red pencil fell out of Zoe's hair, and she stooped to retrieve it. "I-it's complicated."

"The work you and Veronica did there is wonderful. She has three-fourths of a book—"

"The rest will come."

"Why can't you just talk to her?"

"Because I...I..."

There was a brisk knock at the door.

"I have a little confession," Ursula began hastily.

A slim, blond woman dressed in a sedate black silk suit stepped inside.

"Did you ta-a-lk her into it yet?" came that all-too-familiar Texas drawl.

"Veronica!" Zoe whirled on Ursula and met her boss's stern, chocolate dark eyes.

Ursula raised her brows again. "She begged me to talk to you. I have a better idea. Since she's come all this way, why don't you two just use my office to talk and get this little disagreement settled?"

"Little disagreement?" Zoe whispered, putting a shaky hand on the swivel chair behind Ursula's desk to steady herself.

"You'll both feel better, and I have a meeting—"

"Ursula, don't you dare leave me with her," Zoe pleaded.

Ursula picked up her purse and briefcase and glided out of her office.

"Do you like it?" Veronica patted her blond hair that was secured in a demure knot at her nape. "The new...subdued me?"

"You may look subdued. But you're faking it."

"Why aren't you with him and Noah?" Veronica asked.

"Who, Anthony? You know the answer better than I do."

"But we didn't— We didn't do anything— He wouldn't—"

"He wouldn't? I don't believe you."

"You don't believe in yourself any more than I

believe in me. Maybe that's why I can work with you so well and we somehow stumble into our little literary miracles.''

''He didn't?''

''And I was bad, too.''

''Those thong panties—''

''I don't remember taking them off. I swear. That ouzo stuff… No more drinking, my therapist said. No more men, either, until I get myself together. And I've stuck to that…ever since Rhodes. I'm really sorry, Zoe. Sorry I messed things up between you two. I met Noah. He's darling. He needs you. I'm sorry about Noah, too. And sorry I messed things up between us.''

''Do you understand that saying you're sorry doesn't mean anything when you keep doing the same thing?''

''I passed out in the restaurant right after you left. All your Anthony did was try to drive me home so I wouldn't get into real trouble, but I wouldn't tell him where the villa was. Not that I'm sure I could have found it anyway. When I tried to seduce him, he told me he loved you, that he always had…even when he was married—''

''He really wouldn't do anything…?''

''How many times do I have to tell you that. He was a perfect gentleman. He was protecting me because I was your writer. He was loyal to you.''

Zoe raced past her.

''Where are you going? What about my book?''

''Put that cute tail of yours in your chair and write it. Write anything. Believe in yourself. It'll come.''

''But—''

''Just do it. You've written four bestsellers.''

"Not without you! Stop! Where are you going—"

"I have a phone call to make and a plane to catch."

"Where—"

"Vegas. I'm getting married."

"Does Anthony know?"

"I'm fixing to call him and propose. Right now."

"Oh, great! This is great!"

"What?"

"My ending! All this passion! It's coming! I can feel it!" Veronica threw herself into Zoe's arms.

"It's called self-confidence. I didn't do anything to help you find your ending. You just got your mind off your fears. Which is what you just caused me to do. I was afraid to believe him. Afraid to believe in me. Afraid to love."

"You're really something," Veronica whispered, squeezing her tightly.

"So are you."

"I will never ever make a fool of myself and hurt you over a man again."

Zoe hugged her back. "Okay. I forgive you. But you'd better get your act together—you hear. Next time, you'll be toast."

"One question—can I be in the wedding?"

"Now, that's pushing it. That's definitely pushing it."

"Remember—believe in you."

The rain had just about stopped outside as Zoe sat down at her desk and pressed her cordless telephone against her ear.

"Vegas?" Anthony murmured slowly, not really

comprehending. "Why in the world would I meet you in Vegas?"

"You proposed."

"You said no."

"I wish I hadn't."

His end of the line went quiet. "I was just reading something you wrote about me in Greece and threw away," he finally said. "Noah dug it out of your trash can."

Suddenly she could barely breathe.

"I thought you hated me until I read this."

Oh, dear. Now he knew how desperately she loved him. "Yes or no, Anthony?" she whispered. "Will you marry me?"

"Are you serious? You're talking forever? You were pretty upset in Greece and determined never to see me again…even if you loved me. You said love made you too vulnerable to hurt. You went into how much you'd loved your parents and how devastated and lost you felt when they died and that you never wanted to be hurt like that again. That if you didn't let yourself get really close to somebody, you couldn't hurt like that. Then in New York, you turned me down again. What changed your mind?"

"Because I love you. I always have and I always will. I just have to start believing in me and in us, that's all. I let my insecurities get the best of me. Maybe we'll be lucky. Maybe I won't ever have to face losing you."

"I'm glad you called. I damn near killed myself on a bronc awhile ago. My life isn't worth much to me without you."

"I know the feeling."

"What about being an editor?"

"I can freelance from Texas. Maybe I'll even write something other than...personal drivel."

"Hey! That stuff was good."

"Just because now you see how out of control I am about you."

"I like knowing that. So, you're really serious about us?"

"You're all that matters. You're everything. Oh...and Noah. I can't wait to talk to Noah."

"He's right here."

As Zoe held the receiver and waited for him to find Noah, she felt so completely loved. They weren't even married, but she already felt as if Anthony and Noah were her family.

Love. Magic lived in that simple word.

Noah's voice burst against her ear. "Oh, boy! Are you really going to be my new mommy?"

Her heart swelled. She nodded as tears of happiness streamed down her cheeks.

"You know what? Nana said that sometimes fortunes come true."

"Fortunes?"

"Fortunes in fortune cookies."

"And ours did come true," he said. "I got a new mommy and Daddy got you."

"Oh, Noah, I can't wait to see you!"

"Daddy wants to talk to you again."

"There's something I want to know," Anthony said when he got back on the phone.

"Anything."

"Did you and Uncle Duncan... Was he able to consummate the marriage?"

"I don't know. He wouldn't tell me."

"How..."

"I have absolutely no memory of our wedding night."

"I swear on all that's sacred, our wedding night will be a night you'll remember."

"Then, no ouzo," she teased.

Epilogue

The newlyweds' penthouse suite had gilt walls, red carpet and stunning views of Las Vegas. The king-size bed was surrounded by lavish floral arrangements.

Zoe snuggled closer to her new husband. Moving her body against him lazily, she trailed a fingertip down his nose.

"You are so handsome. I still can't believe you're all mine," she said.

"Believe it."

"Just like I can't believe you made love to me all night," she whispered.

"You were counting…"

"To make it last. I still feel tingly."

"I did all the work."

"Don't complain. It was fun."

''Boy, was it.'' He fingered a tendril of her auburn hair.

''I can't believe every single citizen of Shady Lomas sent us flowers.''

Anthony's dark face broke into a grin. ''The shady lady of Shady Lomas isn't shady any longer. She's married to the right man, and she's a new mom to boot.''

''I wonder where Noah is right now.''

''Veronica had better be minding him around those damn slot machines.''

Aunt Peggy and Henrietta had rented a huge suite of their own. Along with Veronica, they were supposed to be taking turns keeping tabs on Noah. The plan was that one of them would baby-sit while the others went downstairs to play the slots. Only, Noah was fascinated by the bright, noisy casino, especially the slot machines that spit silver dollars, and he kept following whoever went down to the casino.

''I still can't believe you let Veronica fly in and be your maid of honor,'' Anthony said.

''She explained everything. She said you were the most incredible gentleman.''

''How come you believed her and not me?''

''Maybe I was so miserable without you, I was ready to listen. Being stubborn wasn't paying off too well, you know.''

''I couldn't believe how restrained and ladylike she was during the ceremony. Her suit came all the way up to her neck. And she's so good with Noah.''

''It's the new her. And no ouzo. She says she adores children. Plus, she's in therapy.''

''Good. Deep down she's probably a wonderful person.''

''Oh, she is.''

''You're the one who's really wonderful.'' Anthony kissed his wife's mouth and then her cheek.

Passion burst inside her. ''No,'' she whispered playfully.

''What?''

Zoe wrapped her arms around his broad shoulders and climbed on top of him. ''This time I'm going to do all the, er, work.''

He didn't complain when she deftly brushed her lips down his throat and then moved her head lower, much lower.

''You know I dreamed of making it big in New York, of proving myself to you,'' she said. ''Funny, how being married to you and kissing you makes me feel that all my dreams have finally come true.''

''Mine, too,'' he whispered huskily.

''I believe in you and me.''

''It's about time.'' He pulled her into his arms and rolled on top of her.

''I thought you didn't want to do all the work,'' she murmured.

''I changed my mind. I love you. Oh, I love you so much.''

She grinned. ''I love you, too.''

''We're going to have a wonderful life,'' he promised.

''I know,'' she agreed. ''I can't wait.''

''So, who's waiting?'' he whispered.

They kissed each other and clung as if to make this special moment last forever.

Then he let her go and stared into her eyes and smiled.

* * * * *

If you enjoyed
A COWBOY & A GENTLEMAN
you will love Ann Major's next few books:
SHAMELESS
Available from Silhouette Desire June 2003
and
THE HOT LADIES MURDER CLUB
Available from MIRA Books, Fall 2003
Don't miss these fast-paced stories
from an exciting author!

COMING NEXT MONTH

#1483 THE PLAYBOY & PLAIN JANE—Leanne Banks
Dynasties: The Barones
Gail Fenton was immediately attracted to her boss, gorgeous Nicholas Barone, but she assumed he was out of her league. Then suddenly Nicholas seemed to take a much more *personal* interest in her. Was she wrong, or had this Cinderella finally found her prince?

#1484 BECKETT'S CONVENIENT BRIDE—Dixie Browning
Beckett's Fortune
While recovering from an injury, police detective Carson Beckett tracked down Kit Chandler Dixon in order to repay an old family debt. But he got more than he bargained for: beautiful Kit had witnessed a murder, and now she was in danger. As he fought to keep her safe, Beckett realized he, too, was in danger—of falling head over heels for sassy Kit....

#1485 THE SHEIKH'S BIDDING—Kristi Gold
The Bridal Bid
Andrea Hamilton and Sheikh Samir Yaman hadn't seen one another for years, but one look and Andrea knew the undeniable chemistry was still there. Samir needed a place to stay, and Andrea had room at her farm. But opening her home—and heart—to Samir could prove very perilous indeed, especially now that she had their son to consider.

#1486 THE RANCHER, THE BABY & THE NANNY—Sara Orwig
Stallion Pass
After he was given custody of his baby niece, daredevil Wyatt Sawyer hired Grace Talmadge as a nanny. Being in close quarters with conservative-but-sexy-as-sin Grace was driving Wyatt crazy. He didn't want to fight the attraction raging between them, but could he convince Grace to take a chance on love with a wild cowboy like himself?

#1487 QUADE: THE IRRESISTIBLE ONE—Bronwyn Jameson
Chantal Goodwin knew she was in trouble the minute Cameron Quade, the object of her first teenage crush, strolled back into town. Quade was the same, only sexier, and after what was supposed to be a one-night stand, Chantal found herself yearning for something much more *permanent!*

#1488 THE HEART OF A COWBOY—Charlene Sands
Case Jarrett was determined to honor his late brother's request to watch out for his widow and unborn child. The truth was, he'd secretly loved Sarah Jarrett for years. But there was a problem: She didn't trust him. Case knew Sarah *wanted* him, but he had to prove to her that her fragile heart was safe in his hands.

SDCNM1202